ALL THE AFTERS

WILD FIRE SERIES

J.H. CROIX

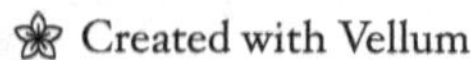 Created with Vellum

Chapter One

TISH

I rested my elbows on the railing, letting my gaze arc over the river below. The water seemed almost ethereal, impossibly blue water fed by a melting glacier. I slowly inhaled, savoring the crisp, cool air. I could've sworn the air here was fresher than any air I'd ever breathed in my life.

It felt as if I was in the middle of nowhere with mountains towering in the distance. I could almost forget about the narrow two-lane highway behind me. Considering that I'd been born and raised in a city, it really *did* feel rather nowhere-ish. Alaska, the land of fresh starts, at least for me.

I was the only person at this little viewing rest stop. The railing was tall, higher than my waist. Glancing down, it was obvious why. Below was a rocky cliff that angled almost straight down to the edge of the river. Part of me wanted to strip off my clothes and dive into the water below.

Holding my arms wide, I twirled in a half-circle and let out a joyous greeting. The sound of my voice echoed back to me. "Hello-hello-hello-o-o-o-o!"

"Hello," a man's voice came from behind me.

I shrieked and spun around. Standing before me was a man so handsome and rugged, it was as if Alaska had delivered him up to me on a platter. He had rumpled, dark blond hair with flickers of gold in it that glimmered under the bright sunlight from above. His eyes were silvery-gray. Tall with broad shoulders, he wore a faded navy-blue T-shirt that clung lovingly to his muscled chest, paired with well-worn black jeans and black leather boots.

"I didn't see you here!" I yelped.

"I gathered," he said dryly. "It's worth saying hello to the world here. I've done it myself." His lips kicked up in a half grin that sent my belly tumbling into a spin.

I wasn't sure why, but there was something a little familiar about this man. I mentally thumbed through my recollections, wondering if I'd met him somewhere before. That made no sense though. I was in the middle of almost-nowhere Alaska, and it was the first time I'd ever been here.

When my eyes shifted toward the truck that must've pulled up while I was staring at the river and the mountains, I noticed that he had Alaska license plates, so he had to be local.

I didn't get a bad feeling, but I sure hoped he was safe. I didn't know what I would do if he wasn't. I'd already discovered cell phone reception was seriously spotty in Alaska.

I managed to smile back at him, feeling my cheeks heat as he took a few steps closer. He approached me almost as if he were aware that maybe I was feeling cautious.

"Have you ever been to Alaska?" he asked.

I noticed his eyes flick toward my vehicle, the

Chapter Two

GRIFFIN

The woman in front of me barely seemed to hear me. One moment, her pretty hazel eyes were focused on my face, and the next, she whispered, "Oh no."

I could tell she didn't hear my question. Sensing she was about to faint, I reached her just in time and she slumped into my arms.

"Well," I said to myself as I looked down at her.

Her eyes had fallen closed. She had silky brown hair pulled back in a ponytail. She wore a fitted blouse that flared around her hips over a pair of fitted jeans that tucked into, you guessed it, fitted boots with low heels.

I adjusted her in my arms and carried her toward her car. She must have had her key fob on her, because it automatically unlocked when I stopped beside it. Except, I couldn't just leave her in her car. That didn't feel right.

I turned to walk toward a small bench. It was nothing fancy. Roughhewn planks on two logs situated against a stone wall. I sat down, easing her to my side, while keeping my arm curled around her shoulder, so she didn't topple over in the opposite direction.

She was pretty in an understated way. Her nose endearingly tipped up at the end. Her lips were full, in contrast to the sharp lines of her face. Her cheekbones rose high and her jaw had a clean, angled line. I noted that she wasn't wearing a ring on her ring finger. I had no idea why I would even notice that detail.

The few minutes I'd spent in this woman's company had been electrifying. When I pulled into the viewing area for a break and to stretch my legs, she was standing by the railing, looking out over the glacial river. I might've not even said anything until she let out her joyful shout and spun in a circle, appearing ecstatic to be here.

While I did love Alaska and meant what I said when I told her it was amazing, the last few months of my life had been challenging and I was weary inside. I'd taken this drive, starting with a short ferry ride, from my hometown of Fireweed Harbor all the way up to Fairbanks solely because I wanted some peace and quiet. There was more than enough of that here. Miles upon miles of empty stretches of highway with few other cars in sight, and wildlife sightings aplenty with only the occasional human encounter.

It had been maybe a minute or two since I'd carried her over here when I felt her shift against me and glanced down to see her eyes opening. After she blinked, her gaze was clear again. She sat up, blinked a few more times, and let out an annoyed huff.

"Are you okay?" I repeated my earlier question from right before she fainted.

She sighed. "I'm fine. I have this weird thing. They call it syncope. Basically, sometimes I get lightheaded and faint. It never happens when I'm sitting down, which is the only reason I'm allowed to drive."

"Ah, I see."

She straightened more fully. I was a little disappointed to lose the press of her soft curves against my side. "Thank you," she said as she looked around. "I'm assuming you kept me from face-planting and carried me over here?" She peered up at me.

"Yes, and no need to thank me. I'm a firefighter. It's in my wheelhouse."

"Catching random women when they faint and carrying them to benches?" she asked, her eyes teasing.

"Sure, if that's what the occasion calls for."

As we sat there smiling at each other, I experienced a sense of lightness. There was an ease to sharing space with her.

Her gaze broke from mine first. She stood up and brushed her hands down the front of her jeans before tapping her palms together lightly. "Well, I should get going."

I didn't want her to leave. "Do you mind if I ask your name?"

She studied me quietly for a few beats before offering, "Tish."

"What would you say if I wanted to call you?"

A light gust of wind came off the river, blowing her ponytail in a swirl.

"I would say that I don't know. What's your name?"

"Griffin."

I wasn't sure why I chose to leave out my last name, but I did, just as she had.

"How about if we ever see each other again, we can take that as a sign?"

Chapter Three

GRIFFIN

A few years later

My brother Wyatt held his wife's hands and looked deep into her eyes. "I do. I do," he repeated for good measure.

My throat was tight. I was happy, in a bone-deep way, for my twin brother. He'd crushed on Rosie for years before he'd been crazy enough to dare her to get a marriage license when they were in Las Vegas.

Roughly a year later, they were still happily married, but they were doing a recommitment ceremony. I glanced around the room to see plenty of teary eyes and lots of smiles. My mother had her palm pressed to her chest.

Rosie said her vows before Wyatt laid a deep kiss on her. The assembled group let up a small cheer. A few moments later, I clapped him on the shoulder as he turned to hand me his jacket. He'd worn a suit and everything. He'd said he wanted to get this seriously right. Wyatt could be a tad superstitious.

"I'm happy for you," I said, leaning close to his ear. He glanced over. "Yeah?"

"Well, I was already happy for you because you're already married," I teased. "But this is good. You wanted it, Rosie wanted it, and Mom is beside herself. Now, make sure you keep treating Rosie right."

He flashed a quick grin before he turned his focus back to his beaming wife. The party swung into full gear. The ceremony was at the park down by the harbor. With it being summer, the weather was gorgeous. Of course, that wasn't always the case, but today, the weather obliged the ceremony with a bright blue sky, sun glittering on the water, and a soft, salty breeze coming off the harbor. The winery restaurant was catering for the reception. Once the ceremony was over, food and drinks flowed.

Tourists milled about nearby as well. Fireweed Harbor was one of Southeast Alaska's popular travel spots. Boats rolled in and out of the harbor, both fishing and recreational. A raft of otters frolicked near the shoreline and a pair of curious seals watched us as they swam nearby.

"You're the only one left," my sister commented from my shoulder.

I glanced over at McKenna. "What do you mean?"

"You have to get married next."

I stared at her. "I'm in no hurry," I finally said.

McKenna took a bite of a crab puff. While she was chewing, I stole two of them and popped them in my mouth. "Wow, these are so good."

"Can't go wrong with Alaskan king crab and cream cheese," she said dryly. After finishing another crab puff, she added, "You should be."

"I should be what?" I countered.

When we got to the top, Wyatt and Kenan were there on the docks and helped both of us up.

"We need blankets now," I barked out.

I lifted her in my arms and began striding down the dock. Someone from a nearby boat came clambering off with some towels and blankets. As I looked down into Tish's wide, frightened eyes, my heart gave a startling kick.

Chapter Four

TISH

I could feel the water dripping from my dress. I was freezing cold and still a little in shock that I'd even ended up in the water.

"Tish," a low, rumbly masculine voice said.

I stared up into a pair of startling silver-gray eyes. They were like a stormy sky. Discombobulated as I was, it took me a few beats to realize why I recognized the man holding me. "Griffin?"

My pulse was galloping like a horse out of control. I tried to say something else, but my teeth were chattering. My lips were so cold I couldn't form another word. I was dimly aware of his strong hold. This was now round two for this man rescuing me. Of all the days to see him again, it had to be this one.

"She's bordering on hypothermic," he said to someone.

As the warmth of his body started to seep into mine, I realized we were encircled by people. I heard feet pounding on the dock, followed by Griffin barking out orders about getting a blanket and something else.

I was disappointed, almost bereft, when he eased me to my feet and someone else wrapped a blanket around my shoulders. My awareness gradually became sharper.

Griffin was busy telling everyone what to do. Sometime later, he was standing at the back of the ambulance where they'd situated me.

"How are you doing?" he asked.

One of the EMTs commented, "Her temperature is in the normal range now. Once we got her wrapped in one of the heated blankets, she warmed right up. I don't think she needs to be assessed further. We just need to find her some dry clothes."

Griffin's eyes bored into mine, and my heart flipped over in my chest. Someone appeared with clothes, and the next thing I knew, the female EMT helped me change into a dry sweatshirt and a pair of soft cotton pants and socks.

"Do you know where your shoes are?" she asked.

"Uh, at the bottom of the harbor," I said, feeling together enough now to smile sheepishly.

She chuckled. "Good point. Hang on, I'm sure we can rustle some up."

I should've known walking on the docks wasn't a good idea. I was accustomed enough to occasionally having my little episodes that they didn't bother me too much. Somewhere along the way, I'd explained to the EMT that I had a syncope disorder. We agreed the icy cold water was what made it such an issue today.

A few minutes later, I was wearing a pair of slightly too large running shoes. The EMT asked me if I needed a ride home.

I shook my head. "I'm all set. Thank you. Is there anything else I need to do?"

I was uncertain about the order of events when

I couldn't even focus on the secondary compliment. "Rhys Cannon is your brother?"

"He sure is."

I let out a wondering laugh. "Wow. And here I never thought I'd see you again."

In hindsight, that explained why Griffin had looked a little familiar when I first saw him. I'd wondered about that detail since. While I hadn't seen him before then, I'd seen his brother, who shared a clear resemblance.

"You did say if we saw each other again to take it as a sign," he pointed out.

My belly did a little flip. "I guess I did."

I didn't even know what to do with any of this. At all.

Griffin seemed to pick up on how unsettled I was and smoothly shifted the topic away. "How are you doing now?"

"Fine."

"You're warm enough?"

"Yeah. The water *was* freezing, but I'm okay. I definitely don't plan to fall in the harbor again."

He chuckled. "Do you remember what happened?"

I usually didn't worry about explaining this, but Griffin had already seen me faint. This was round two. "My brain skips a beat sometimes and I faint. I just wanted to walk out on the docks. Next thing I knew, I felt it coming on. I should've known better. The last thing I remember is wondering if a sea lion would eat me."

My heart sped up a little at the rumble of his chuckle. "Not likely. Not impossible, but humans aren't really their preferred meal."

"Thank you for diving in and rescuing me."

"Anytime."

"I hope I didn't ruin the wedding reception."

"Of course not. Now there's a story."

"What do you mean?"

"When something goes perfectly, there's not much to say about it other than how perfect it was. But when something goes wrong, preferably a harmless mishap, there's a good story to share later."

I snorted. "I suppose."

The pharmacy came into view, and Griffin slowed to turn down the side street, the sound of the blinker loud in the quiet that had fallen between us. A moment later he pulled around the back of my small apartment building. My job came with a reduced rate on this apartment. The apartment was small, but nice and furnished. I loved it.

He parked, and before I could say anything, he'd fetched the bag with my dress out of the back and was waiting for me when I climbed out of his SUV. "You don't have to carry that up," I said.

He looked at me quietly. "Are you sure?"

I felt my lips curling up in a reluctant smile. "Griffin, you literally saved me from drowning today," I pointed out. "I can handle carrying this into my apartment."

We studied each other for a moment, and I felt tiny flares of heat shooting up inside. His gray eyes flashed silver. He looked remarkably like his brothers. They shared similar features, a straight nose, a strong jaw, and full lips. He was the only brother I hadn't officially met. All six of the Cannon brothers were objectively handsome, and yet not a single one had elicited anything beyond a vague appreciation from me. Until Griffin. Apparently, being rescued by him, not once, but twice, had created a storm of chemistry inside with little bolts of lightning zapping through me.

He handed over the bag with my dress in it with a dip of his head. "There you go. I'm sure I'll see you again soon."

"I'm sure," I squeaked. I tried to ignore the little jolt I experienced when his fingers brushed against mine as he handed the bag over. It felt like fire streaking up my arm.

I didn't realize I was just standing there, clutching the heavy bag until he prompted, "Tish? Did you need something else?"

"Oh!" I almost jumped. "No. Thank you again."

He studied me for a beat before he nodded.

I spun around and hurried into the entrance to the building, turning back to call out, "Thank you!"

"For fuck's sake, how many times do you need to say that?" I whispered to myself. Flustered, I rushed into the building.

I hurried past the reception area to the small bank of elevators. This was a newer building, luxury housing in the heart of Fireweed Harbor, or at least that's how it was described when I looked it up before I moved here.

I took the elevator up to my floor, fumbling to tap the code into the keypad at my door before I walked in. I dropped the bag by the door, feeling the shaky jitters that were still reverberating in my system as I dashed into my bathroom.

When I lifted my eyes to look in the mirror, I let out a resigned laugh. My hair was drying in wild curls, my mascara was streaked, and I looked like a big mess.

Chapter Five

GRIFFIN

"How's Tish?" I asked my brother as I walked into his office a few days after the reception.

Rhys, my oldest brother and the CEO of our family's corporation, looked up from his desk. "Fine."

I wanted to press and get more details, but I didn't. I'd randomly stopped by just to see if she was here. She wasn't, but then, I didn't have a plan if she had been.

"What are you doing here?" Rhys asked.

"Just thought I'd stop in to say hi."

"You know, any day you want to stop doing the firefighter gig..."

I shook my head. "I like my job, and I'm not really an office kind of guy."

Rhys studied me for a beat as he leaned back in his chair. "I know. Whenever you decide you're too old to risk your life on the regular, you can work with Kenan." Kenan was another older brother who handled most of the odd jobs for the corporation, so he was all over the place.

"I could use a quick breakfast. Want to walk with

me to Spill the Beans Café?" Rhys stood from his desk, hooking his hand on the jacket draped on the back of his chair.

"Always." I fell into step beside him as we walked down the hallway and outside into the chilly morning. Hoarfrost was covering the landscape, creating a glittery shimmer as the sun's rays began to melt the thick, spiky frost. The days were getting shorter with time rolling past the end of summer into autumn. The sky was strikingly blue, a contrast to the slate gray water. The sun struck the water at an angle, illuminating it with streaks of gold shimmering over the surface.

I zipped up my jacket as we walked. "How is it going with your crew?"

My twin brother Wyatt and I had been on a hotshot firefighter crew in Fairbanks for over five years. Wyatt had moved back to our hometown a little earlier than me to take over the head brewer job at our family's brewery and winery, part of Fireweed Industries, the heart of it because it's what started the entire corporation.

When a new hotshot firefighter expansion crew was temporarily stationed here, I took the chance to come to my hometown for a while. It might not be a permanent place for me, but it was good to be here. The rest of my siblings had migrated back once Rhys moved the corporate headquarters from Seattle back to Fireweed Harbor. It was a strategic choice now that the business no longer needed to be located in an urban center with the flexibility offered by the online world.

Wyatt and I didn't discuss it much, although we were a lot more open these days, but some of the secrets and darkness in our family's past had been busted into the open. Messy though the process felt, it was best for all of us.

"Glad to be here?" Rhys asked as we walked.

My breath misted in the air. I cast him a quick glance as I nodded. "I am. It's working out well. I get to do what I love and be here for the time being."

Fire season was winding down, but these days, fire season stretched longer, and our crew traveled wherever we were needed. Lately, there were more and more wildfires with hotter summers and more unpredictable weather.

Rhys threw me a quick grin. "Feels good to have you here."

I nudged him with my shoulder as we walked. I glanced to the side as we walked past the harbor. Living in Alaska, Fireweed Harbor specifically, felt like living in a postcard at times. The picturesque harbor glittered under the early morning sunshine. Boats were bobbing in the water, and an eagle screeched nearby with a seagull calling in return.

"We need to take a detour," Rhys commented.

I looked ahead to see a moose ambling across the road up in front of us. We immediately turned down a short side street. The moose had fully crossed the street when we came back onto Main Street and turned onto the small walkway that led to Spill the Beans Café.

Even though it was early, the café was full with most of the tables occupied when we walked in. Warm air scented with baked goods and coffee assailed us as the door swung shut. As soon as we got to the front of the line, Phyllis smiled up at us. She and her best friend Hazel owned this café together. I was convinced they knew everything about everyone in town. In fact,

I was positive they ferreted out details about myself before I even knew them.

"Well, hello, boys," Phyllis said, her gray curls bouncing with her smile.

"Hey there, Phyllis," I replied. "So, you're on duty this morning? I thought you handled the afternoon."

She rested a hand on her hip. "I will have you know I cover morning duty plenty. Rhys can confirm this."

Rhys chuckled. "Confirmed."

Just then, Hazel appeared through the swinging door that led into the bakery area in the back. As soon as her gaze landed on Rhys and me, a grin stretched across her face. "Hi, boys!"

"What's with everyone calling us boys?" Rhys teased.

I nudged him with my shoulder. "Rhys is the CEO of Fireweed Industries. Give the man some respect."

Hazel rolled her eyes as she stopped at Phyllis's side. "I've known both of you since you were infants. You're boys to me. Deal with it."

"Excellent point," I offered.

"Plus, when it comes to toughness, Griffin is the toughest," Phyllis teased.

Rhys nodded vigorously in agreement. "Damn straight. You won't catch me putting out fires out in the middle of nowhere."

"And, what's this thing they're talking about now? Zombie fires?" Phyllis asked, her eyes shifting to me.

"Those are fires that never really go out. They smolder underground during colder months and pop back up later," I explained.

The bell jingled on the door behind us, just as Hazel asked, "What can we get you two?"

Rhys glanced over his shoulder. "Oh, there's Tish. I'll cover hers."

I might've guessed it was Tish based on the prickle of awareness that rose on the back of my neck.

I glanced over when she stopped behind us. Rhys stepped to the side, gesturing her forward between him and me.

He studied the bakery display case. "Are those lemon muffins?"

Phyllis nodded. "Lemon *filled* muffins," she said with emphasis.

"They're really a pastry disguised as a muffin," Hazel added.

I chuckled. "Kinda like a doughnut with filling, but it's a muffin?"

Tish let out a muffled laugh, and I glanced toward her. "You know you want one."

Her cheeks went a little pink when she looked up at me. "Actually, I do." She looked over at Rhys. "And, you don't have to pay for mine."

"I'm getting it for you," he insisted. "Hazel won't let you pay for it." He narrowed his eyes at Hazel.

Hazel chuckled. "It's a work expense for him, Tish. I am sure you go above and beyond for Rhys all day long at the office."

Rhys's wife, Haven, appeared through the back door. She used to work here and often stopped in to chat and occasionally fill in in a pinch. She heard the tail end of Hazel's comment, interjecting, "I don't know what I would do without Tish. She saves me every day."

Rhys looked affronted as he glanced from his wife to Hazel to Phyllis and Tish. "I don't make Tish work too much."

I chuckled. "From what I hear, Tish makes it so you don't have to ask for anything. You forget we all had to put up with your venting back before you had an assistant when you were in Seattle." I glanced to Haven. "Have we ever told you how stressed out he was back then?"

Rhys let out an aggrieved sigh. "I worked too much, and I should've gotten an assistant much sooner."

Tish stayed quiet through all of this. I glanced down at her, teasing, "You're a smart woman. Stay out of this."

Her eyes widened slightly.

Smart woman, ha! My mind taunted me.

A smart woman wouldn't have the hots for her very important boss's brother and one of the family members who technically owned the corporation where I worked, even if he didn't work there at the moment. This was, by far, the best job I'd ever had. I most definitely didn't want to screw this up. My life was financially stable and peaceful, and I wanted to keep it that way.

I smiled up at Griffin, trying not to literally burst into flames under the heat of his gaze. A moment later, Rhys handed me the coffee and muffin that I had tried and failed to pay for.

"I should—" I began.

Rhys cut in, "I don't mean to interrupt, but you don't have to hurry into the office early. It makes me feel like I'm a slacker with you getting there before me every single day."

Haven, who also worked for Fireweed Industries, smiled over at me. "Do whatever you need to do,

Tish." She glanced to Rhys. "If I were her, and you were my boss –"

Griffin interjected, "You *are* kind of his boss." He winked at Rhys.

Haven rolled her eyes, not missing a beat, clearly accustomed to the banter between the Cannon family siblings. "Anyway, my point being, it's probably relaxing and quiet to get to the office a little early. It's usually very busy. Coffee with us means she's sort of on duty."

Rhys smiled down at her. "Good point."

"I just have a few early calls to make. Thank you for the coffee." I said my goodbyes and began to depart, just as I heard Griffin's voice. "I need to get rolling. I have a meeting at the fire station. I'll catch you guys later."

I heard the chorus of goodbyes and lengthened my stride slightly as I slipped through the door. I studiously kept my gaze ahead, as though I didn't feel Griffin's presence like a blast of heat from behind.

The seconds ticked by before I felt him catch up to me. In order to keep ahead of him, I would practically have to run. My stride wasn't nearly as long as his. A moment later, he crested my shoulder.

"How are you doing?" he asked.

I pressed my glasses up my nose as I glanced up to the side. "Fine, you?"

"Pretty good, actually."

"Didn't we just do the polite conversation thing?" My voice was a little tight.

"I suppose. Habit," he said with an easy shrug.

I looked out toward the harbor as we approached it, and I couldn't help my soft gasp of appreciation. With the sun still rising, the mix of clouds above was shot through with shades of pink, lavender, and silvery rays of light. The view was stunning with the colors reflected in the water shimmering underneath.

"Beautiful," Griffin said, his voice reverent.

"It is." I savored the view for another moment before finally glancing up at Griffin. "It doesn't get old to you?" I asked.

"Never. I grew up here so I'm used to it, but nature's beauty isn't something that wears out. At least, not for me. Honestly, I pay more attention to it now than when I was a kid. Living away from here for a little while only makes me appreciate it more."

"Where else have you lived?" My curiosity about Griffin couldn't be stopped.

"Most recently, I was up in Fairbanks for a few years hotshot firefighting. Of course, that's also Alaska and very beautiful, but different. Alaska's so big, geographically speaking, that, even knowing that, it was still a surprise to realize how different Fairbanks is. I went to college in Juneau and I've spent some time in Seattle. Aside from business, we have extended family in Willow Brook and down on the Kenai Peninsula in Diamond Creek."

"So, you've been all over Alaska," I said.

Griffin chuckled and my belly did a little shimmy. "I suppose so. The crew I worked for up in Fairbanks covered the whole state as well. What about you? All I know is you came up here from Seattle when you took the position as Rhys's assistant."

"I grew up in Seattle. I've done a little bit of traveling in the Pacific Northwest, but that's it."

"So you're a city girl." His eyes crinkled at the corners with his smile.

"I guess so. Seattle has a lot of residential areas that don't feel too much like a city, but it's definitely a city."

"What made you want to come to Fireweed Harbor?"

"I wanted to live somewhere more rural. Alaska is one of those places, you know? A bucket list place."

Griffin was quiet as he studied me. As he looked at me, it felt as if fireflies were lighting up inside my body. I was shimmering inside under the heat of his gaze.

I got so flustered that I blurted out, "I should go! I really do need to get to the office." I couldn't move though.

He held my gaze for several more echoing beats of my heart before nodding. He fell into step beside me, and again, I had to force myself not to start running. My nerves were alight with electricity, and I could hardly contain the way it hummed through my system.

He was quiet as we walked. Blessedly, it wasn't far to the office building. A few minutes later, I stopped in front of Fireweed Industries headquarters.

Normally, I had good manners. I knew how to handle the average social interaction, but I felt tongue-tied around him.

Griffin insisted on walking me into the building. He held the door for me, and I slipped past, trying to ignore the sizzle of electricity that raced up my arm from where my elbow brushed against his side.

"Thank you," I said when I glanced up at him.

He was quiet for several beats. "I have to go!" I announced. "Have a great day!" I sounded like an overeager store greeter.

"You too," he said, dipping his chin, his voice a little raspy.

I hurried away, all but running up the stairs to the second floor where my office was inside the executive suite. A moment later, I was in the bathroom, breathing rapidly with my back against the door. This was beyond ridiculous. I didn't need Griffin Cannon to get me all hot and bothered like this.

I didn't even have to go to the bathroom, but I did need to cool off. I rinsed my hands under cold water and dabbed my face with a damp paper towel.

"What the hell is wrong with me?" I muttered to myself before I smoothed a few loose strands of hair back, tucking them into my ponytail where it rested high atop my head.

A few minutes later, I was busy checking my email, the heat generated in my system by the mere presence of Griffin finally dissipating. A few boring emails from HR would do that to a person.

Chapter Seven

GRIFFIN

As I walked out of the building, my gaze arced over the sign for Fireweed Industries, recently updated by Haven. Among other things, she was a graphic artist. She'd updated the logos for all of our various projects. I loved how she'd woven small fireweed flowers in every design.

My thoughts skipped back to my conversation with my twin brother the other day. Wyatt was busy trying to get me to join him at the brewery, or to do anything for our family's business. Yet, he understood better than anyone that I enjoyed firefighting. It suited me. I knew the score. I couldn't do it forever. Wildland firefighting was an intensely physically demanding job, so at some point, I'd need to change course. I'd deal with that when it was time.

A salty breeze gusted off the harbor as I continued walking down the street to the fire and rescue station. I planned to take care of some admin stuff, meet a few of my fellow firefighters, and so on. I shouldered through the door, walking through the main entrance. The woman at the desk was on the phone. She glanced up and held a finger up when I stopped on the other side.

I nodded and spun around, casually looking around the room. The fire station I had volunteered at in high school had been updated significantly. It was easily twice the size now. What had previously been a tiny desk in the reception area was now a large circular desk. The space had huge windows that offered a view of Main Street and beyond to the harbor.

"Okay, all set," the woman said.

Turning back, I smiled at her. "Hey there, I'm Griffin Cannon. I've stopped by, but I don't think I've met you yet."

"I don't think so either. I'm Sassy." She stood and held her hand out, and I reached across her desk to shake it. "I heard you were coming. I'm supposed to set you up with a bunch of HR paperwork. Give me a sec." She released my hand and spun around, running her fingers along a row of files in a cascading stand. "Here you go."

"Are you HR here?" I asked as I accepted the file folder from her.

"Oh, my gosh, no. That's the Juneau people. We're busy here, but we don't have anyone from HR. I'm just the messenger." At my nod, she continued, "I understand you used to volunteer here in high school. I would've been in middle school at the time." She gave a saucy shrug. "It's nice to officially meet you, and you can call me Sass or Sassy."

I chuckled. "Nice to meet you, Sassy."

"Of course, I know who you are because your family is like, you know, a big deal here. I'm just a nobody from Fireweed Harbor. My parents moved here when I was in middle school, so I don't even know if I count as a local yet."

"I'm sure you do," I assured her.

She flashed a smile, her cheeks dimpling. "Well, anyway, just fill that paperwork out. You're welcome to sit here in the waiting area, or you can go in the back. Actually, wait, you have an office. Oh, my gosh!" She spun in a circle, looking around.

A moment later, she thrust some keys at me. "It locks?" I asked.

"Well, I don't think anybody keeps it locked, but it's an option." Sassy gestured for me to follow her.

Bemused, I followed her down the hallway. As I walked behind her, I took in her appearance. She had wild blond curls pulled up into a ponytail. She wore bright blue glasses that framed her big blue eyes. She had a sparkle to her. And yet, for me, it was purely objective, like looking at a pretty sunset. The contrast to my encounter with Tish moments earlier was stark. With Tish, the moment I was in her presence, it was as if there was a wire on the ground between us, shooting up sparks.

Sassy led me through another doorway into a back hallway. She gestured to a few offices before we came to the back area, which had also been expanded considerably. What used to be a small break area with a few workout machines now had a kitchen with a big table, a workout room behind a glass wall to one side, and a luxurious hang-out space with two large sectional sofas and a massive flat-screen TV mounted on the wall.

"If you need to sleep here, go for it. That has a pull-out couch," she explained.

I chuckled as I glanced over. "Good to know. Seeing as I'm on the hotshot crew, I won't sleep here too often."

Sassy grinned. "Let me show you your office."

There were a few guys working out. I waved when I saw Jack Hamilton, my brother-in-law, glance up from where he was currently moving at a punishing pace on the treadmill. I recognized Hudson Fox as well. He was in the midst of lifting weights and dipped his chin in acknowledgment. He was on the hotshot crew, along with Jack.

Sassy stopped in front of an open door. "Here you go. You and Hudson share this office. I guess it's where you meet for... I don't know, stuff." She pointed to another hallway to the side. "That takes you over to the police side of the building. I handle reception and dispatch for everybody though. It's very exciting."

"Uh, it is?" I couldn't help but prompt.

She nodded, her ponytail bouncing. "Absolutely. Yesterday I took a call for the police department about someone who was trying to steal a shed. A whole shed! Only in Alaska." She rolled her eyes. "And then, there are always the moose calls."

Just then, her headset chimed. "I have to take this. Just fill that paperwork out sometime soon and bring it up to me. I'll turn everything in to HR in Juneau for you. You won't have to do a thing."

After she hurried off, I sat down at the table, ignoring the familiar and annoying frustration that started to rise inside me. I *hated* paperwork. There was the typical dread of paperwork, and then there was what I experienced. It was better than it used to be, much better, but even now, whenever I began reading something it always took a minute or more for my brain to orient. It started with a jumble of words. I had reminded myself how to look at them. I would never be one of those people who could quickly scan documents.

It wasn't until I was halfway through middle school

that a more observant than average teacher noticed I was having trouble reading. I had dyslexia and letters tended to cluster together for me, or my brain would mix letters up. Before they figured out the issue for me, school was incredibly frustrating.

To this day, I remembered the meeting with that teacher and my mom. At that point, it was just my mom taking care of us. Our dad had passed away when I was barely old enough to remember him. Our parents had wanted a big family because they'd both been only children. Except they never planned for our mom to be a single mom. To this day, I sometimes wondered if my father had been there, if someone might've noticed sooner how much I was struggling with school. I loved my mom deeply and never doubted she loved all of us, but she'd definitely been overwhelmed. School had felt almost painful at times.

I had started to feel stupid even though I was pretty sure I wasn't actually stupid. I was really good at math, but trying to read left me feeling confused and muddled. Wyatt had helped me. Although I never explicitly told him I was struggling, he'd seemed to know. Thanks to Miss Julie, I'd gotten the help I needed and learned how to compensate.

I still saw Miss Julie around town. Even now, years later as a grown ass man and a firefighter, she still babied me a little bit. Blessedly, I didn't have much to fill out with the paperwork and got it done. Just as I slid the papers back into the file folder, Jack, my sister's husband, came walking into the office. "Hey, hey!"

I glanced up. "Hey, yourself. How's it going?"

Jack's dark hair was damp from a shower. "Doing well. Are you ready to officially start?"

"I am." I tapped two fingers on the file folder.

"Managed to get the paperwork done. How do things roll around here? I understand from the local crew that you guys do town stuff, and training exercises in the winter. I heard the other superintendent is shifting over from the town crew. Hudson, right?" I prompted.

"Oh, yeah. You'll like Hudson. Solid guy." He paused and studied me quietly for a beat. "So you're not jumping into the family business?"

It was a natural question, and I understood it. "For now, this is what I want. I like being outside. I like being in the wilderness. I don't fit too well in an office. I'm sure I'll reach an age where this isn't what I want because it'll be too hard on me. Until then, I help out when they asked me to do projects and the like, but that's enough."

Jack eyed me before nodding. "Makes sense. McKenna keeps telling me she doesn't want to have to worry about me for too long. As you could probably guess, I have mixed feelings about working for your family."

I smiled wryly. "Makes sense. McKenna will worry, no matter what you do."

Jack chuckled. "Probably true."

The sound of footsteps approaching reached us before Hudson Fox appeared in the doorway. He and I were the newest members of the hotshot crew. His experience with hotshot firefighting came from working on a local crew, while I was more familiar with Alaska's landscape.

"Hey there." He hooked his hand on the back of a chair and spun it around before he sat down and rested his elbows on the back of the chair. "We're still short a few people, but I'm glad you're starting next week. There are a few training things we can do, and we're already getting some calls to help with some fires out of state," he commented.

"With winter on the way, the snow and cold help us out up here," Jack offered.

"On the crew up in Fairbanks, we usually did two runs down to the lower 48 to help with other fires during winter," I said.

Hudson was quiet as he studied me. Although there was an intentness to him, he carried himself with a relaxed ease. I didn't get any of the vibes that could occasionally pop up with men in the world of firefighting. There were those guys who were constantly jostling for dominance and trying to be in charge regardless of their role.

Hotshot crews typically had twenty-five firefighters with two superintendents and team leads. Once you were out in the wild, we had to fan out and a clear chain of command was necessary to manage the situation. Anyone who did the work had to have nerves of steel and enough confidence to put themselves in the line of fire, literally at times.

"There you guys are!" Sassy's voice reached us as she appeared in the doorway.

Hudson glanced over his shoulder. "What's up?" he asked.

"Well, there's a car accident out near the glacier due to a rock slide. The town crew could use some extra help. I was hoping –" she began.

Jack, Hudson, and I were standing before she could finish. "Headed out that way," I said.

Hudson clapped me on the shoulder as we walked down the hallway. "Welcome."

I'd dropped my gear off yesterday, so it was a matter of minutes before we were hustling out to a truck. A few hours later, after we helped a very scared couple navigate their way up a cliff and checked them out to make sure they were okay, I headed home. Aside from a few scrapes and bruises, the rock slide had been unremarkable for the couple in the car. Their car didn't survive, but they did because their vehicle only rolled once before landing on a conveniently located ledge.

After a quick shower back at the station, I began my walk home. I decided to stop in at the offices. I could check in with any of my siblings who happened to be around.

Or Tish, my mind taunted me lightly.

Chapter Eight

GRIFFIN

When I stopped at McKenna's office, she was tied up on a conference call. Haven was deep into design planning.

A moment later, I walked into the suite where Rhys's office was. I knew instantly he wasn't there because his door was closed and there was no light shining underneath the door. There was no sign of Tish either.

My brain catalogued details, assessing she must be somewhere nearby because a jacket was hanging on the back of her chair with a purse sitting on her desk. Just as I was contemplating that it would definitely be ridiculous if I lingered here, I heard footsteps in the hallway.

A few seconds later, Tish walked through the doorway. She had a box in her arms, and I reflexively stepped toward her. "Do you need help with that?"

She shook her head and stopped beside the chair in the waiting area to set the box down. "Thank you though," she replied as she straightened.

For a moment, it was as if her mind went completely blank. Her gaze became unfocused.

"Tish?" I took a step closer.

When she didn't reply and swayed a little on her feet, I eased her into the chair beside her, waiting a few moments. As before when I met her on the side of the highway, it wasn't long before her eyes blinked open.

Her gaze focused on me and she let out an annoyed huff. "Ugh." Her voice sounded tired. "Could you bring me my purse?"

I hurried over to fetch it and return it to her. Her hands were shaking a little when she tried to unzip it.

"Do you want me to get that for you?" I asked, sensing she was frustrated that I was even there.

The sound of her swallowing was audible inside the quiet room. "I've got it." She yanked the zipper open and pulled out a bottle of medication.

I glanced around before walking over to the small water cooler and getting her some water from it. A few minutes later, she had taken the medication and drained the small paper cup of water that I had handed her.

I finally asked the obvious. "Do these happen often?"

Tish lifted her eyes to mine. "Not really. I'm fine," she insisted. "Like I told you before, I have these syncope episodes. For me, all they know is I experience a rapid drop in blood pressure. That medication I just took helps with that."

A powerful wave of protectiveness crashed through me. I didn't like thinking about Tish handling these by herself. I didn't want to imagine what could've happened. My mind skipped back to the day she'd fallen in the harbor.

My jaw tightened. I forced myself to breathe in slowly, to shackle the urge to wrap her in my arms, to do everything necessary to keep her safe. I had to remind myself we were sitting in an office and she was perfectly safe.

"Are you okay now?" I finally asked.

She cleared her throat and nodded. Her face was pale and her eyes looked wary.

"Are you finishing up for the day?" I asked.

She gestured to the box in the chair beside her. "I wanted to bring that in before tomorrow morning. I'm scanning in some old files so we can get rid of the paper files."

I eyed the box. "Do you need me to put that somewhere then? Maybe on the floor by your desk?"

The color was returning to her skin. Her lips curled in a small smile. "I can handle it, Griffin, but thank you."

I smiled back at her. "I'm sure you can, but humor me. Just tell me where to put it."

I could tell she was still tired when she gestured toward the floor beside her desk. "Just over there against the wall. I'm doing a box a day. More than that, and I'll lose my mind."

I chuckled. "I can't even imagine scanning papers all day."

"That's why I do a box a day, so it's not *all* day."

I set the box where she directed me. She was standing when I turned around. I walked to her side quickly. "Take it easy..."

"I *am* taking it easy," Tish protested. "I just let you carry that box over there."

I rolled my eyes. "Fine. Can I walk you home?"

Tish studied me for several beats. The air around us felt as if it was shimmering with sparks. I had to contain myself, to resist the urge to step closer and run my hands over her, making sure she was safe. Of course, she was safe. It was just this feeling of wanting to take care of her was unfamiliar to me.

She let out a breath, tipping her head to the side. "You're going to insist, aren't you? Well, maybe not that, but you'll worry if I don't let you."

When she smiled a little, I felt my own lips curling in response. "Yes. You just fainted."

"I'm fine now."

"What if you'd fallen in the harbor and no one was around?" I pointed out.

"Oh, my God," she muttered under her breath. "You can walk with me. If you insist. Let me get my jacket."

"Go right ahead." I gestured toward her desk chair.

She was wearing a fitted skirt with a blouse. I could tell she was feeling mostly back to herself as she strode with purpose past me and around her desk. I tried to ignore the way her blouse pulled tight across her breasts as she pushed her arms back to slide into her jacket in one motion before shrugging it up over her shoulders. She quickly zipped her jacket up, and I ignored the way disappointment shafted through me. She checked to make sure her purse was zipped before looping it over her shoulder and rounding her desk again.

She stopped beside me. "Shall we?"

As I looked down at her, my mind catalogued the way she had a single loose strand of hair falling down along her cheek. I wanted to brush it back and kiss her. Competing with that was the urge to hook my finger through the elastic holding her ponytail in place and slide it loose to watch her hair fall around her shoulders.

I did none of those things. "Yes."

Our footsteps were quiet in the carpeted hallway. She jogged down the stairs quickly, and I checked the urge to ask her if she was feeling okay again. I held the entrance door as she slipped past me. When it fell shut, she glanced back, making sure it closed fully.

"Do we need to do anything else?" I asked.

Although I knew the combination to get in and out of the building, I didn't actually know if there were special guidelines for closing up after hours.

Tish shook her head. "Nope. It's automated. I just always make sure the main door completely closes. Maybe I don't need to, but..." She shrugged.

"Good habit to have. I would do the same thing."

The air was cooler than it had been earlier. With it being fall, the temperatures could drop quickly. Tish tipped her face up toward the sky, taking a deep breath as we began walking.

"I love the air here," she said. "I swear it's fresher, crisper maybe."

I slid my gaze to hers. "I think it is. Certainly fresher than Seattle or any city. Do you like it here?" I asked as we continued to walk down the sidewalk.

Tish was moving briskly, but it was easy for me to keep pace.

"I love it. Alaska is beautiful. And honestly, more than I expected."

"What do you mean?"

"I knew it would be rural, but a plane ride to Juneau is only twenty minutes and that's an actual city. Since Fireweed Harbor is a tourist destination, there's a lot here with plenty of restaurants, some good shopping, and a good grocery store. All of that with an absolutely amazing view and a quieter life even during the busy times of the year."

"Yup. A lot of people don't realize how even the smaller towns have lots to offer here."

It was only a few minutes before we reached her apartment building. She stopped on the sidewalk in front of the entrance. "You don't need to walk me upstairs," she said.

"Tish, you just fainted a few minutes ago. Let me walk you in. Please."

Tish pressed her lips together and rolled her eyes. "Okay."

"Thank you for humoring me." I held the door as she walked inside.

Moments later, she closed her apartment door. She gestured in a circle. "See, I'm inside and I'm completely fine." Her lips twitched.

"I see that," I said lightly. "I hope you can understand why I might've been worried."

She shrugged, but looked away.

"You fainted. Again," I pointed out.

"I have a syncope disorder. It's part of my life. They don't happen too often."

"How long have you had these?"

"Since I was a teenager. I have these occasional clusters. It's nothing dramatic."

"I don't like it," I stated.

Tish rested her hands on her hips, narrowing her eyes. "I don't precisely like it either. It's just my life."

It was obvious that she was completely okay now. Her eyes were shooting sparks, and her cheeks were flushed. Once again, I was startled at my body's reaction to her. I wasn't thinking when I took a step closer.

I mirrored her, resting my hands on my hips loosely and narrowing my eyes. I felt my lips curl into a slight smile as we stared each other down. For a few beats, her eyes widened before she burst out laughing and her hands dropped from her hips.

Her laugh was low and raspy. Heat whipped through me, need sinking its claws in deeper.

"What's so funny?" I chuckled as my own hands dropped from my hips.

"I guess we're having a stare-down."

Her laugh petered out. Her gaze was bemused when she leveled her eyes with mine again.

We were maybe two feet apart. I could feel the echoing beat of my heart down to the soles of my feet. I took another step closer. "Tell me something," I heard myself saying.

"What?"

"If I told you I wanted to kiss you, would you want me to?"

Chapter Nine

TISH

If I told you I wanted to kiss you, would you want me to?

Griffin's question ricocheted through my thoughts. I stared into his smoky gaze and tried to take a breath. My lungs seemed to have forgotten how to function. I felt lightheaded, breathless, and hot and tingly all over.

Aside from my lungs forgetting their job, my brain was filled with static, and my belly felt all fluttery. I definitely wasn't thinking when I took a step closer to him.

I finally managed to suck in the tiniest bit of air as I stared up at him. With my brain completely offline, I breathlessly whispered, "Yes, I would."

"Would you want a kiss right this minute?"

My head bobbed up and down. I didn't know who moved first, but we moved toward each other, erasing what little distance was left between us. Griffin was tall with broad shoulders. His entire presence was one of strength and protectiveness.

I felt encompassed by his strength. I cataloged details about him. The way his dark blond hair had flickers of gold like burnished sunshine. The little flashes of silver shimmering in his gray eyes. The bold, straight line of his nose, the sharp angles of his cheekbones, and the square edge of his jaw. Even his lips were delineated. Nothing about him was soft. He was all masculine.

As the seconds ticked by, my heartbeat began echoing through my entire body. I lifted my hand and placed it on his chest. I could feel the hard thump of his heart against my palm, and the warmth of his chest through his cotton T-shirt where his jacket was hanging open.

His eyes stayed locked with mine. It felt as if he was searching, almost reaching right into me, and grabbing a hold of me, kicking away my defenses, latching onto a thread of need, of wishfulness, of vulnerability and holding on tight.

I felt the electrifying brush of his fingers along my cheek just before he smoothed a lock of hair away. His touch simmered over my skin, leaving sparks dancing on the outer shell of my ear. His fingers trailed like a flame down the side of my neck. His thumb dragged along the edge of my jaw. I felt as if I were tumbling into the moment with a fire burning through me, liquid all over as I stared up at him.

All he had done was touch me, and barely. When his thumb dragged over my bottom lip, I was near to breathless. My lips parted as I shifted on my feet, restless from the storm inside. Heat rampaged through me and a tightness curled in my belly.

"Griffin," I heard myself whispering.

The pleading tone of my voice should've shocked me, but it didn't. My pure want for him was too powerful.

"Yes?" he whispered gruffly.

"Kiss me. Please." I felt the clench between my

thighs and shifted again on my feet, trying to relieve the pressure building everywhere.

"Okay," he whispered over my lips.

His kiss started soft and questioning. I unconsciously made a sound in my throat, needy and pleading. My entire body felt shockingly alive, with my pulse thrumming along at a breakneck pace. Every tiny sensation fed into the others, creating a breathless intensity.

Griffin paused, lifting his head, just enough to create a pocket of space between our lips. I was distantly startled at the little whimper that slipped out from the back of my throat. I wasn't one to feel desperate, to feel bereft when there was a pause in a kiss.

And yet, Griffin had that effect on me. He elicited a sense of desperation inside of me.

"Are you sure you want this?" he rasped.

With each word, his lips touched mine. Every point of contact felt like a spark of electricity landing on my lips.

"Yes." That single word was emphatic.

I let out a sigh of sheer relief when his mouth came to mine again. It was a tease, a soft brush of his mouth over mine before he dusted kisses on the corners of my lips. I made a sound of impatience as I shifted closer, savoring the feel of his strong, muscled chest against me.

That seemed to spur him forward. One of his arms slid around my waist, his palm landed at the dip in my back where my hips flared outward. His fingers curved over the top of my bottom. The low sound in his throat sent a sizzle of electric fire through me.

He slid his other hand into my hair as he angled my head to the side and fit his mouth over mine. Our kiss went from a brushing tease to commanding. I *loved* it.

I took another step closer, erasing the millimeters between us. One of my hands mapped his chest, and the other curled around his waist, dipping under his jacket and the hem of his shirt to feel the banded muscles along his back.

His tongue tangled with mine in slow sweeps. I didn't even know if I was breathing. I felt made of liquid need. I was trembling by the time he lifted his head. His dark eyes bored into mine, and it felt as if I was staring into silver smoke. He didn't step back, still holding me close. His hand loosened its grip in my hair and slid down to rest at the base of my neck.

I was acutely aware of every single sensation. The pads of his fingers on my skin, where his other palm had slid down a little further over my bottom, the press of his body against mine. All the while, my mind was filled with static.

I tried to slow my breathing, but my heart was rampaging wildly. I experienced a small sense of relief to feel his heart thumping hard and fast underneath my palm.

His shoulders rose, his chest pressing against me as he took a deep breath. "I should go," he said, even though he didn't move at all.

I wanted to ask him to stay, but I didn't. This was a folly, a reckless moment. Because I knew better, or at least I hoped I did. But if I'd known better, I wouldn't have even let this happen.

When I didn't say anything, Griffin stepped back slightly. "Tish?" There was a lilt of a question in his voice.

I had to clear my throat to even speak. "Yes?"

"What do you want?"

I startled myself by answering with blunt honesty. "I don't want you to leave."

The heat banked in his dark gaze flared. I could practically see him trying to make a decision. "I don't want to leave either, but I think maybe I should."

Just then, my body decided to make its other needs known and my stomach audibly growled. I giggled when Griffin's eyes widened before crinkling at the corners with a slow smile.

"I should've asked if you needed to stop and get something for dinner," he said.

"Obviously, I'm hungry," I pointed out.

He was still holding me with one arm around my waist. My palm was still against his chest.

"What if I stay for a bit and we order some takeout?"

Before I could think better of it, I was nodding, and saying, "Sounds like a plan."

I sensed his reluctance as he slowly stepped back.

"What do you want?" I asked.

"Other than you?" His intent was clear.

Heat blasted through me and I shifted on my feet again because I could feel the moisture between my thighs. This was *so* not me. I just wasn't like this with men. Ever.

I took an unsteady breath. "I meant, what do you want to eat?"

"Whatever you want. I can get us something from the winery restaurant."

"That sounds perfect. I'm not really in the mood for pizza, but I could absolutely go for one of those sesame chicken sandwiches."

He nodded. "I'll order."

———

By some freaking miracle, I managed to keep it together. Of all the things I had imagined doing this evening, it didn't include the hottest kiss of my life with Griffin, followed by an ordinary, casual dinner.

Griffin was polite, and even insisted on helping clean up. He washed the dishes quickly. It was only two plates and two glasses. And yet, my eyes lingered on the way his forearms flexed when he handed me the second plate.

That was how bad I had it for Griffin Cannon. I was on the verge of drooling over his forearms. Moments later, he turned and rested his hips against the counter. His gaze caught mine. "When can I see you again?"

A simple enough question, but it flustered me. I wasn't supposed to be kissing Griffin. I certainly wasn't supposed to be having dinner with him. I definitely wasn't supposed to be contemplating how I could handle the awkwardness of dating my boss's brother. Even though Griffin didn't work at the company, his family owned it. I wasn't an idiot. I knew I'd be skirting a line if I let things go further.

I moved my hands around in the air pointlessly before asking, "Do you think that's a smart idea?"

Chapter Ten

GRIFFIN

Several days later

"You want me to what?"

"Go to Willow Brook and help Chase and Archer out while they get the new brewery up and running," Rhys said pointedly. "If you want to stay there when you're done firefighting, you can take over as head brewer there. You and Wyatt can coordinate."

I studied my brother for a beat. "I have an actual job, you know."

"I know, but we're headed into winter. I know from your schedule before you won't be working straight through winter. I figure in between training, or when you're off duty, maybe you could help out with this. Tish can be your main contact here to coordinate."

Tish's question from the other night echoed in my thoughts. *Do you think that's a smart idea?*

She had gone on to point out she worked for my brother, and she didn't want to put her job at risk.

"Isn't she your assistant?" I hedged.

Rhys nodded. "Of course, but she does special projects for me. That's part of her job. She knows better than anybody in this company the background of what needs to be set up administratively. She'll coordinate with HR and get everything dealt with. She'll hire all the admin staff there. I trust her more than anyone to handle that."

"What about Kenan or McKenna?"

"Neither one of them likes dealing with hiring. Kenan is too impatient for it, and McKenna is a total softie. Tish is organized and practical. You can help out with that and help Chase and Archer get everything lined up there. They have a location opened, but we don't have the restaurant started yet beyond events, and we're shipping beer and wine from here to there."

"They can't travel here?" I hedged.

Rhys rested his elbows on his desk, steepling his fingers together under his chin. "If you don't want to do this, I understand. Chase and Archer both have young kids, so it's better for them to stay there full-time. You have a little more flexibility. I had hoped you could help in your downtime. I will not pressure you to officially take any of those jobs permanently."

I didn't want to say it aloud, but this was perfect for me. Winter was the off-season for hotshot firefighters. I never liked being bored. Yet, I felt pulled by opposing forces. Knowing that Tish would be my primary support on this project made it almost irresistible. But I knew she might not like that idea.

This wasn't a problem I could discuss with Rhys because he would tell me to back the fuck off around

Tish. I decided to do the logical thing. "Okay, I'll make it work."

"Talk to the crew at the station, let me know when you have some in-between times, and we'll schedule your travel."

At that moment, there was a light knock on Rhys's office door. "Come in!" he called.

I knew it was Tish before she even opened the door. For me, the magnetism of her presence could reach straight through the door.

"Oh, I didn't mean to interrupt," she said, as soon as her eyes landed on me.

She was composed. With her hair pulled back tightly, she wore a fitted skirt and a silky blouse that fell to her hips. My mind conjured up the image of her blouse unbuttoned and that skirt rucked up around her hips while I teased her. I forcibly kicked my thoughts off that track. Fuck me.

"You didn't interrupt," Rhys replied. He gestured her through the door. "I was just speaking with Griffin about a project for us. He's going to help out when he has time in between firefighting this winter with some things at the brewery in Willow Brook. I'd like you to be his main contact here."

Tish's eyes flicked from Rhys to me and back to Rhys. There was the barest hint of a flush on her cheeks. "Of course." The phone rang out in the reception area. "I'd like to get that if you don't mind," she said.

Rhys waved her away with a smile. "Answer the phone."

Tish gave me a quick nod, giving nothing away in her gaze.

That was the last time I saw her. For months.

Chapter Eleven

TISH

Griffin: *Hey, I haven't seen you in the office at all. Hoping everything is okay.*

I stared down at Griffin's text and let out a sigh. Though a part of me wanted to be a coward and just ignore him, that didn't feel right. And yet, I most definitely didn't have the courage to tell him the whole truth.

Before I could chicken out and overthink it, I tapped to open the text screen and replied.

Me: *Dealing with some family things. That's why I haven't been in the office. I think you already know this, but it's really not a good idea for me to see you. I'm not sure when I'll be back in the office.*

As soon as I hit send, I didn't block Griffin, but I muted him. It had been three weeks since that stupid kiss. I rested my elbows on my kitchen table and tried not to cry. I was beyond startled with the direction my life had taken.

I tapped my phone screen again, this time pulling up the screen into the portal for my doctor's office. I wasn't lying when I said I was out of the office because of family things.

"Oh, my God," I muttered on the heels of a shaky breath.

Three months ago, before I'd seen Griffin again and discovered he was my boss's brother, I'd been dating a guy. I met Paul through a dating app, the scourge of modern humanity. He'd seemed like a nice enough guy, nice enough that we went on multiple dates. In a startling and pleasant surprise, he hadn't sent me dick pics. At all.

I shook my head every time I thought about the overwhelming number of dick pics offered up by guys on dating apps. I'd liked Paul enough to go past kisses, and then that fated night happened.

That night had been the first time in a long time I'd done something other than kissing with anyone. We had all of the responsible conversations about birth control, expectations, and so on. He wore a condom. Until he didn't. The sex had been nothing more than okay. I was cautious about all the shitty things men could do, spiking drinks and more. Hell, in college they'd gone past spiking drinks to carrying around needles to jab girls with date rape drugs. I thought I'd been so on top of it. I did all the things to make sure Paul was safe. I'd checked his background, checked his work history, and so on. Not a single red flag came up. Until he slipped the condom off right at the end. By the time I realized what had happened, it was too late.

He made a show of getting up to dispose of the condom after we had sex. But I was no idiot. I felt the semen running down my legs between my thighs when I stood.

"Did you take your condom off?" I asked.

Paul with his rumpled dark hair and nice brown eyes glanced over, not quite meeting my eyes. "It must've slipped off." His tone was too casual.

I'd known in that very moment that he was lying. With my stomach churning and a discombobulating sense of betrayal rocking me. I'd stared back at him while I stood there naked. "I need you to leave."

"Now?" His eyes widened.

"Now."

I'd made myself vulnerable with him. I'd felt safe enough to actually have sex with him. I hadn't had sex with anyone since my college boyfriend.

Every time I thought about it, which was far more often than I wished, a sense of shame and embarrassment rolled through me. It took a lot for me to let my guard down. I'd gone and done it, and now Paul was nowhere to be found and I was pregnant.

I didn't want to see him again. *At all*. I'd actually been relieved when I heard he left town for a commercial fishing job. My stomach roiled at the reality that I was pregnant. I knew I needed to make a decision. On the list of things I hadn't really thought about when I moved to Alaska was the state of reproductive rights. I hadn't thought it would be something I needed to worry about. A quick Internet search revealed Alaska protected abortion in their constitution and had even before the recent national upheaval.

Although I didn't know what to do, it was a relief to know I had a choice. I was startled to discover I didn't know if I wanted to have an abortion. I most definitely didn't want to try to parent with Paul. I couldn't trust him at all and couldn't even imagine rebuilding trust.

My gut already seemed to know what my brain wasn't quite ready to accept. I wanted to have this baby even though the situation felt like a little bomb dropped in the middle of my life. It would most definitely blow my life up.

I was still trying to figure out what to do about work. Rhys had graciously agreed to let me work remotely while I handled my "family matter". He was a good boss. I felt betwixt and between about what to do about Griffin. Rhys had no idea how I had met Griffin. He certainly had no idea that we had kissed, and I intended to keep it that way.

Chapter Twelve

TISH

I read Rhys's email for the third time. He wanted me to write up a job description for HR. My eyes scanned over the salary figure. Rhys paid me well as his executive assistant, but this position paid substantially higher since it was a management position. I wanted it. The job would take me out of Fireweed Harbor and it would give me the income bump I needed.

My fingertips hovered over the keyboard. Making a change like this would take me *way* out of my comfort zone, but I wanted this chance. Before I could overthink it, I reached for my phone. Rhys answered on the second ring.

"Tish, please tell me you're ready to come back to the office." I could hear the smile in his voice.

I hesitated for a beat before forging ahead. "Actually, I was hoping I could come in and meet with you, so I could explain what's going on."

Although it was late in the afternoon, I knew Rhys would still be at the office. He was better about managing his schedule since he had fallen head over heels in love with Haven and they had a baby. Yet, he still worked a solid hour past when the office closed.

"Of course. I'd love an update. I hope everything's okay."

"It is," I assured him.

A short while later, Rhys eyed me from across his desk. He steepled his hands, tapping his fingertips together as he studied me. I knew he was surprised by my request about the job. "Of course, I support that. Obviously, I'll be really disappointed to lose you as my assistant, but I want what's best for you."

"I hope it is. I appreciate your faith in me," I said.

"Rather than draft the job description for that position, how about you write one for your current job?"

I smiled over at him, a rush of emotion tightening my chest. I really liked working for Rhys, and I genuinely appreciated his support.

"Happy to. If you'd like, I'll help screen applicants for my position. The one thing I wasn't clear about is the time frame for this management position."

"Whatever works for you. It's a new position in Willow Brook, so it's not as if we're dealing with a vacancy. I assume you'll need time to get moved, and we should talk about your plans for taking leave," he replied.

I'd decided I needed to tell Rhys about my pregnancy. I needed to make plans, so I felt like it was best to share that sooner rather than later. I'd left out the shitty way it came about. Paul was nowhere to be found. With a few casual questions around Fireweed Harbor, I'd learned he planned to move back to California after his commercial fishing stint ended. I'd sent him a text, letting him know that I was pregnant and planning to have the baby. I had no idea if he had even read it. I didn't intend to file for child support and didn't want him involved.

"How do you feel about all of this?" Rhys asked.

I pondered his question. "Afraid, nervous, excited, so many things."

"You can handle it, Tish. Are you telling anyone else about your plans?"

"Just my parents so far."

He nodded. "You know our leave policy. You can have six months of paid leave. If you'd prefer to take it all at once, just let me know. I'll put you in touch with my brother Chase and my cousin Archer. They both live in Willow Brook and work for us. They can give you some leads on housing. I would imagine with their help you can have a place lined up within the month. You can do your work remotely while you handle the transition. With a baby on the way, I think it's best if you get moved sooner rather than later."

"I don't have to take leave—" I began.

Rhys narrowed his eyes, his hands dropping to his desk. He shook his head forcefully. "If there's one thing Fireweed Industries tries to do right, it's taking care of our employees. Since it's a new position, I think it'll be less disruptive for you to take leave. You will need it and your baby will need it too."

I almost burst into tears as I stared over at Rhys. "Thank you." I pressed my palm to my chest. "I know this is a big change for me in the company, but I'm looking forward to taking on more responsibility."

His eyes crinkled with his smile. "I completely support it." Just then, there was a knock at his door. "Come in!" he called out.

Before the door fully opened, I knew it was Griffin walking in. I forced myself to take a slow breath. I did not need to react to my boss's brother. So what if we kissed? It didn't matter. I was having a baby and moving and starting an entirely new phase of my life.

Griffin stepped into the office, his gaze instantly locking with mine. Heat rose swiftly into my cheeks, and I had to force my eyes away from him.

"Hey there," Rhys said, hopefully oblivious to my reaction to his brother.

"Hey," Griffin said. "I was just stopping by to see if you'd be going to locals' night."

Rhys's eyes shifted up to the clock. "That's the plan."

My brain felt filled with static. I lost track of what Rhys was saying until he said, "...and Tish will be transitioning to the new management position for the Willow Brook location."

"Oh?" Griffin prompted.

My eyes swung to him. I cleared my throat as heat suffused my entire body. I felt fidgety and restless.

"Yes. It's a great opportunity for me," I squeaked.

Chapter Thirteen

GRIFFIN

"I thought Tish was irreplaceable as your assistant," I said to Rhys.

He spun his bottle of beer in his fingers on the table, nodding in agreement. "She'll be difficult to replace, that's for sure. But she wants this new position and she'll be excellent at it. She deserves the salary increase too."

I literally had to grit my teeth to keep from suggesting he just bump her pay to match it. That I even contemplated that train of thought was ridiculous. I didn't completely understand it, but it was clear Tish wanted to keep her distance from me. I would have to respect that.

"Hey, hey!" I glanced over my shoulder to see my twin brother Wyatt stopping beside the table. He tugged a chair out and sat down beside me.

"Hey, yourself," I replied, as he nudged me with his shoulder.

"What's up? You look a little—" Wyatt tipped his head to the side as he studied me.

"Tired," I offered.

I didn't doubt Wyatt likely knew there was more to it than that, but he let it slide. "Sure, tired."

Before he could say more, a waiter arrived at our table. I was relieved for the busyness of the evening. As usual, my whole freaking family was there. There was lots of chatter, and Rhys broke the news that Tish would be moving to Willow Brook.

Haven smiled over at him. "I hope for all of our sakes that she finds a good replacement for herself as your assistant."

"She will," Rosie, Wyatt's wife, chimed in. "Tish *is* really good at her job. She can find someone else who's really good at the same job. I have faith in her."

"When is she moving?" Haven asked.

"I'm going to put her in touch with Archer and Chase. Probably within the month. If they can help her find housing, which I'm sure they can, she can do her job here remotely as we start the search to fill her position here. We'll make it work," Rhys explained.

I found myself glancing around the restaurant a few times, wondering if Tish would actually be here. I never saw her that evening.

———

Two weeks later

I rounded the end of an aisle in the grocery store, glancing up to see Tish perusing the vitamin section.

"Hi, Tish," I said.

Her head whipped up, glancing toward me. "Oh!" she squeaked, her cheeks flushing pink. "Hi."

She had her purse over one shoulder and a basket

looped over her other arm. Her hand tightened around the strap of her purse.

"Getting ready to move?" I asked when my eyes landed on the packing tape in her basket.

"Uh-huh," she said.

I wanted to say more, to press on why she was so insistent about keeping me at a distance. "Well, I travel to Willow Brook a few times every year. I might see you there sometime. Rhys had mentioned me helping out with the brewery there, but it sounds like that might be covered by the staff already there. I suppose you won't have to worry about coordinating with me on that." I paused, wondering what else to say. When she stayed silent, I added, "Anyway, good luck."

She opened her mouth as if to say more before snapping it shut. She cleared her throat and swallowed. "You take care, Griffin."

I watched her walk away, feeling like there was something big I was missing about the situation.

Chapter Fourteen

TISH

Over a year later

"Buh-buh, ga-ga..."

"Hi, my baby boy." I gave my son a smacking kiss on the cheek. At five months old, his babbling repertoire was increasing by the day.

He giggled and my heart almost ached with love. When I had decided to have a baby, I'd been unprepared for how it would feel. Even though I felt overwhelmed literally *all* the time and as if I was flying blind through being a single mom, I didn't regret my choice, not even for a second.

With Teddy, who I'd named after my father Theodore, just past five months, I was ramping up to go back to work full-time. I'd already been working part-time from home for the last two months. I didn't have to work, but I found it difficult not to. It gave me a little structure and I needed that. Rhys had been incredibly accommodating with my schedule, but I was more than ready to go back to a regular work schedule.

Although I was going to miss being with Teddy all the time, I wanted to work. I missed it. I especially missed talking to adults more often.

I gave Teddy another kiss and began to get everything ready to drop him off for his first full day at daycare. Having a baby meant I was always carrying what felt like *all* the things.

I was forever grateful to my friend Phoebe, who had given me many pointers about trimming down what I needed to carry when I went out and about. I'd met Phoebe through Rhys's cousin, Archer. She and Archer were happily married and had been a huge help to me when I moved to Willow Brook.

A few minutes later as I was walking out of the small house I rented, my neighbor Madison happened to be walking over from their house. She and her husband lived next door, just through a small cluster of trees.

She stopped to wait for me in the driveway. As soon as I reached her side, she gave Teddy a kiss. "Want me to get him in the car seat for you?"

"As if I'd say no," I teased.

Madison chuckled as she smoothly shifted him from my arms into hers. In addition to help from Phoebe and Archer, Rhys's brother Chase and his wife Hallie had also been incredibly helpful. Maybe it would've worked out anyway, but during a completely overwhelming time in my life, I was beyond grateful for the support.

I'd met Madison and Graham through my new connections since Graham was a firefighter on the crew Chase used to work on. Graham had kept the home he lived in before he and Madison married, and when the previous tenants moved out, Madison had let me know. The price was affordable and I loved it.

"Thank you so much," I said as she buckled Teddy into his car seat while he babbled at her.

"Babies are the best," she said as she gave Teddy another kiss and smoothed her hand over his downy soft hair.

Graham appeared along the trail through the trees that led from my house over to theirs just as Madison was closing the back door to my car.

"I thought you must've walked over here," he said, his eyes twinkling.

Madison smiled up at her husband as he stopped beside her. He was a strapping hotshot firefighter, handsome and completely besotted with Madison. With her glossy black hair and striking green eyes paired with a kind and generous personality, it was no wonder Graham adored Madison.

Graham leaned down and brushed a kiss on her cheek, and I almost felt as if I was interrupting them by the intensity in his eyes.

"Oh, Dad, get a room!" Allie's voice reached us. Allie was Graham's college-aged daughter and Teddy's favorite babysitter. She babysat for me and took care of Madison and Graham's toddler son whenever they needed help.

Graham straightened, glancing over to his daughter and chuckling. "I just kissed her on the cheek."

Allie rolled her eyes dramatically. "I know, but the PDA is *much* sometimes." Pausing beside my car, she reached for the handle on the door. "Can I give Teddy a kiss?"

"Of course," I said with a smile. Teddy adored Allie.

She opened the door, and Teddy giggled and

gurgled, kicking his feet against the bottom of his car seat. When she closed the door a moment later, I glanced at the three of them, tears stinging at the back of my eyes. My life had felt flipped upside down before I moved here. It was sometimes beyond overwhelming, and yet they, along with other new friends who had welcomed me into their world, had made it much smoother than I could've anticipated.

Allie slid her hand through my elbow and squeezed. "When do I get to babysit again?"

"Anytime," I said.

"I'm working today," she said.

"He's going to daycare," I explained. Allie's brow furrowed with worry. "He's been doing three hours at a time there already. He's going to be fine," I said, more for myself than her.

"Meet me for coffee?" Madison asked before I climbed into my car.

"When?"

"After you drop Teddy off. You're going to need it before you go into work."

I smiled. "I'm still nursing, so no more than a cup a day for me, but I'd love to." I waved to them as I drove away.

A short while later, I dropped Teddy off at daycare and managed not to cry. Even though I wanted to be at work, it was still hard to know he was going to be there for a full eight hours. I drove the short distance from his daycare down Main Street to Firehouse Café, smiling when I saw Madison's car in the parking area. When I pushed through the door into the café, Madison was waiting in line with two other friends, Phoebe and Tiffany.

"Hey again," Madison said.

Her gaze encompassed Phoebe, Tiffany, and me.

"Tish just dropped Teddy off for his first full day of daycare."

Phoebe gave me an understanding smile. "That's a big day."

"I'm ready. I miss working full-time, and I can't believe I'm saying that. I'm going to miss being with him all the time, but..."

"Hey, you're talking to me. I can't even—" Phoebe paused and shook her head. "Full-time mom-ming is just not for me. I am not the homemaker type."

"Well, you used to be a firefighter," Tiffany said. "Although, I can't imagine the full-time mom thing either. It's harder than work."

I burst out laughing. Madison said something just as the door to the café opened. I didn't know how I knew, but my body knew that Griffin Cannon had just walked in. A shiver of awareness skated over my skin. *It can't be him.*

I heard another man's voice and let out a silent sigh of relief. It wasn't Griffin. But when I glanced over my shoulder, Griffin was walking beside Beck Steele. My radar for Griffin was accurate. Beck was holding his wife's hand. Maisie had also become a friend. Her dark curls were bouncing around her shoulders as she laughed at something Beck said.

My breath seized in my lungs when they stopped beside our group. Beck gestured amongst us. "This is Griffin Cannon. He's on the crew from Fireweed Harbor that's being relocated here."

Voices piped up with introductions, while I was trying to remind my lungs how to work again. I'd known Griffin might show up in town. Aside from the fact I worked for his family's corporation here, he had a cousin and a brother who lived in Willow Brook.

Yet, I'd put him so far out of my mind. Denial was maybe not a healthy coping skill, but it worked.

Griffin's eyes locked with mine, and I felt the heat flash into my cheeks. "Hi, Tish," he said in that voice I'd never forgotten.

"Hi!" I squeaked.

"Oh, you two know each other?" Beck prompted, glancing between us.

Griffin was more together than I felt. "Of course. Tish works for Fireweed Industries. She used to be my brother's assistant before she moved to Willow Brook."

"Uh-huh." My barely audible reply came out sounding strangled.

Maisie caught my eye. While there's no way she could've known just what Griffin represented to me, she seemed to know I needed someone to rescue me from this moment.

"Oh, another firefighter. Like we're short on them around here," she said dryly.

Griffin glanced her way, his lips curling with a quick smile. "Surely you can always use another."

At that moment, Amelia Masters approached with her husband, Cade. Amelia was another friend I'd made since moving here. Amelia sort of intimidated me. She was tall, leggy, beautiful, and tough. She ran a construction company with her best friend. She seemed like the kind of woman who had it together in every way that I didn't.

"You must be Griffin," she said when she stopped beside Maisie.

Griffin glanced to her. "I am, but how did you guess?"

Cade chimed in, "Beck texted us he was taking you here for coffee."

Madison grinned at Beck. "You should know that Beck is the gossip around the fire station."

"I am not a gossip," Beck said, lifting his chin. "I share pertinent information."

Maisie burst out laughing, nudging him with her elbow. When I got to the counter, Janet James was smiling across at me.

"Hi there," she said warmly.

Janet had been so welcoming when I moved to town. She tended to mother-hen, and I'd needed that kind of comfort and support.

"Hi, Janet. I'll take my usual please," I said.

I felt Griffin's presence at my side. It felt as if a wall of heat blasted my side. I glanced at him briefly, willing the blush to dissipate from my cheeks as I gestured from him to Janet. "Janet, this is Griffin Cannon. He's one of the new firefighters in town. I know him from Fireweed Harbor."

Janet's eyes twinkled as she smiled at Griffin. "I heard about that crew being moved here." She flicked her braid off her shoulder. Janet was soft and round with a weathered face with an ageless quality to her. Her hair was dark and streaked with more salt than pepper. "I do hope you'll enjoy Willow Brook."

"I love it here," he replied. "My brother Chase lives here, along with my cousin Archer."

Archer appeared as if on cue. "Hey, hey!" He gave Griffin a quick hug.

Stepping back, Griffin replied, "Good to see you."

"You came here before you stopped by our house," Archer teased.

"I just got into town. I told Beck I'd stop by the station and he brought me here."

I was relieved when Griffin got drawn into conversation with several of the firefighters. I got my coffee and slipped away to sit at a table with Madison, Phoebe, and Amelia. Maisie said her goodbyes as the rest of the group filtered out.

I had taken a few sips of coffee when Madison asked, "So, what is the deal with you and Griffin Cannon?"

I almost spit my coffee out on the table. Amelia patted me between my shoulder blades. "Are you okay?"

I cleared my throat and took the napkin Phoebe offered me from my side. After a moment, I glanced around the table, wondering how to get out of this conversation.

Madison narrowed her eyes. "Don't even try with me."

"Try what?" I countered, keeping my tone light.

Phoebe's grin was sly. "Something happened with you and Griffin."

I let out a sigh. "Griffin and I almost dated. And, we kissed once," I finally said.

"That must've been one hell of a kiss," Amelia said, waggling her brows.

I bit my lip, trying to ignore the heat rising in my cheeks. "At the time, I was his oldest brother's assistant. I was worried about the work thing. I kissed Griffin maybe a week before I figured out I was pregnant. I wasn't seeing Teddy's father by then." I rolled my eyes. I still felt embarrassed and ashamed about what had happened. "I hadn't seen him for over two months by the time that kiss happened with Griffin."

I still felt a little sick every time I thought about it. "Teddy's father is an asshole. I got pregnant because he took his condom off. I didn't know it had a name, but it's called stealthing. I thought he was a nice guy, but he wasn't. It's not like I thought it was going to be forever, but..." I shrugged. "I confronted him and he left town."

Madison had heard this story before and the warmth in her eyes helped me through the moment.

"You decided to have a baby, obviously," Phoebe said practically.

"I did, which kind of surprised me. I don't doubt it, or regret it for a second. I've never even heard from the guy again. I texted him about it, and he never replied. Pretty sure he blocked me completely," I explained.

"So, you kissed Griffin, found out you were pregnant, and...?" Madison circled her hand in the air.

"You never lose the thread," I teased. "I found out about this job and asked Rhys if I could take this position. I would've been interested anyway. The pay is better and it's a management position."

"Totally makes sense," Phoebe said. "Archer is thrilled you're here." Archer was one of the executives for Fireweed Industries in Willow Brook.

"Does Griffin work for Fireweed Industries?" Madison asked.

"He could, but he says he likes being a firefighter," Phoebe chimed in. "He says he wants to do that until he's too old for the work."

"What are you going to do about Griffin? Because that man *totally* has a thing for you," Madison said.

"I don't think he has a thing for me. It's been almost a year and a half since I've seen him."

"Oh, he *totally* has a thing for you," Amelia offered wryly.

"Seriously?" Although I was acutely aware of my hormones' happy reaction to Griffin, it was hard to believe he'd still be into me.

"He could hardly keep his eyes off of you," Madison said.

Although my little heart had other ideas, I tried to stay practical. "I'm a single mom and I can't do a relationship. I doubt he even knows I have a baby."

"Of course he knows," Phoebe said. "You've been on maternity leave. Do you think his brother wouldn't mention it?"

"Well, I guess I was hoping there was no need to talk about me," I mumbled before taking a sip of coffee.

Amelia chuckled at my side. "This will be fun. We haven't had this kind of gossip around town in a while."

I looked over at her. "I refuse to be the subject of town gossip."

"You already are," Madison said with a sly grin.

When I got in my car to leave a few minutes later, my phone vibrated with a text.

Griffin: *I understand congratulations are in order. I'd love to see you.*

Chapter Fifteen

GRIFFIN

I stared at the text I'd just sent to Tish before I forced myself to push my phone away. I wasn't usually the kind of guy to dwell on a woman. I had other priorities, including a job that took me away often, family, and more.

And yet, Tish lingered along the edges of my thoughts and had ever since the first time I met her. I'd thought she'd remain a distant, passing memory in my life. Until it turned out the job that brought her to Alaska was for my family's company. Just when I thought I might have a chance with her, she'd moved and I'd heard she was pregnant. Questions swirled in my thoughts about who the father was.

"Hey," a voice said from the doorway.

I glanced over from where I sat on a bench in the locker room at Willow Brook Fire & Rescue. I had more than one reason to take this position here. I could've told myself it was because I had family here. When I'd learned they were relocating the hotshot crew to Willow Brook with the other crews here, I'd jumped on the chance. Because Tish was here.

There was that and the opportunity to take over managing the brewery location our corporation was starting here when I was ready to call it quits with firefighting.

"Yeah?" I stood from the bench and reached for my jacket in the locker behind me.

"Want to catch some dinner?" Hudson Fox asked.

I hesitated because I didn't know if Tish would reply to my text. But then, I could always dip out if she did.

"Sure."

Hudson flashed a smile. "Excellent." He ran a hand through his shaggy dark hair, his green eyes bright in contrast. "You've been to Wildlands before, right?"

"Sure have. I've stayed there when I visited family before."

I fell into step beside Hudson as we began walking down the hallway.

"You've probably been to Willow Brook a lot, huh?" He stepped through the door into the parking lot before me, holding it open as I walked through.

"We've certainly visited plenty," I began.

My brother Chase chimed in, "Hey there."

"Hey, hey," I returned as we exchanged a quick hug.

Chase had been a firefighter for years. He had a baby at home now and had shifted over to the local crew so he wasn't traveling as much.

"Thought I'd try to catch you. Figured you'd be walking over to Wildlands," Chase said.

"Good guess," Hudson commented.

Not much later, I was enjoying a beer and a burger with a few fellow firefighters and Chase. "Not on toddler duty tonight?" I asked after I finished the last bite of my burger.

My brother chuckled as he shook his head. "I will

be tomorrow though. Hallie's got an event at the gallery tomorrow." His wife was a professional photographer. He leaned back in his chair. "So, what's the plan for you long-term? You think you'll stay in Willow Brook after you're done firefighting? Can't do that forever, you know."

"That's the plan. I signed a two-year contract for this position. I'll see how I feel at the end of that. Rhys and Blake are hoping I'll take the same role here that Wyatt has at the brewery in Fireweed Harbor," I explained.

Chase took a swallow of his beer as he nodded. "It's a good plan. You can do like me. Settle down, get married and get your adrenaline fix by filling in when they need extra help."

I chuckled, just as I felt my phone vibrate in my pocket. Slipping it out, I glanced down to see a text from Tish. Chase was replying to something Hudson said from his other side, and I tapped to open the text.

Tish: *It would be good to see you. If you haven't heard, I have a baby now.*

I noted the time on my phone. It was still fairly early. Maybe I was showing my cards too soon, but I was impatient to see her.

Me: *How about tonight? I can stop by. With a few nieces and nephews, I've got skills at putting a baby to sleep.*

As soon as I sent the text, I forced myself to put my phone back in my pocket. Maybe I didn't know Tish all that well, but I sensed she wouldn't reply immediately.

When Hudson stood from the table, I followed suit, clapping Chase on the shoulder, and leaning down to say, "I'm gonna head out for the night. I'll see you soon."

Chase glanced up with a nod. "Absolutely. Glad to have you here in town now."

Just as I reached my truck, I felt my phone vibrate again.

Tish: *Ok, if you don't mind. I don't have dinner or anything.*

I was surprised she didn't dissuade me, but we were definitely overdue for a conversation. It wasn't that I thought Tish owed me the story of her life, but I *was* curious about what happened. I knew a little bit from Rhys, but I tried not to ask too much because I didn't want to pique his curiosity about my questions and wonder what the hell was up.

When I eventually began working at the brewery here, I knew I'd see her often. Even though it didn't make sense that I was sort of hung up on her after all this time, I was. Something about her had slipped through the cracks of my defenses.

After she texted me her address, I tapped it into my GPS, arriving there a short drive later. The days were getting shorter, but it was still light when I rolled to a stop at the end of her driveway. Although her house wasn't too far out of town, the area was largely surrounded by trees.

Moments later, I knocked lightly on the door. My heart felt squeezed tight by a fist when I met Tish's eyes.

Her hair was pulled into a messy ponytail. She was clearly stressed. She had a baby in her arms, and he had his fingers curled around some of her falling-down hair. His cheeks were pink and round and he wiggled mightily in her grip.

"I'm sorry," she said immediately. "I thought he'd be asleep by now."

I wasn't even thinking as I reached over. "I'll take him."

Tish's eyes widened in surprise, but she didn't hesitate to pass the baby over to me. Maybe it was pure surprise, or maybe it was that she was clearly tired.

"Hey there," I murmured as I held the plump baby in my arms and adjusted him against my shoulder.

"What's his name?" Maybe I was making assumptions about his gender, but this guy gave off serious boy energy.

"Teddy."

"Hey, Teddy." He wiggled and fussed a little. "Can I come in?" I asked.

"Oh! Of course." She stepped back, holding the door as I walked through.

Whether it was because he was simply shocked to be in someone else's arms, or that I held him in a way that worked for him, Teddy settled after a moment.

I glanced around the place. The door led into a small entryway. The ceilings were high, so the space felt open and airy. The entryway shifted from tiled flooring to hardwood into an open living room and kitchen area. The sun was setting now, leaving streaks of fading gold in the sky above the mountains. I rocked Teddy in my arms and he curled against my shoulder, letting out a weary sigh.

"Are you magic?" Tish teased as she looked at us.

"Don't think so. I learned the knack of comforting a fussy baby with one of my nephews. I'm convinced most of it is not being a tired parent," I offered with a shrug.

Tish let out a soft laugh. "True. Do you want to walk with me to his bedroom?"

"Lead the way."

We walked across the living room to a short hallway. We passed a bathroom on one side, and another room strewn with toys, a playpen, and a desk in the corner. Across the hallway was another door that Tish led me through. It appeared to be her bedroom with a queen-sized bed against the wall and a bathroom beyond that. She led me into a small room off to the side where there was a chair beside a crib.

Tish held her fingers to her lips and gestured toward the crib. "Want me to get him?" she whispered.

I shook my head. I had done the transfer of a sleeping baby into a crib enough that I thought I could pull it off. I knew the less we moved Teddy, the better. He didn't stir as I carefully placed him in the crib. Tish tucked a blanket around him.

We tiptoed out. She left the door ajar and reached for the baby monitor remote on a small table by the bed as we walked out. She didn't say a word until we had made it back down the hallway into the kitchen. She sat down on a stool, letting out a big sigh. "We made it!"

I chuckled and lifted my palm to slap hers with a high-five.

"You are magic. It's obvious you've put more than one baby to bed." She smiled at me, looking almost giddy.

"I wouldn't say it's magic, but I have put more than one baby in a crib. I babysit for my family here and there."

Tish rested her elbows on the counter. "Have a seat."

I slipped onto the stool across from her. "How are you?"

She held my gaze for a long moment before slowly shrugging, looking almost as if she didn't even know the answer. "Pretty good," she finally said. "How are you?"

"Pretty good." I paused, studying her for a moment. She looked tired, but peaceful. "It's really good to see you, Tish."

She held my eyes, her gaze thoughtful. "Is it? I'm sure you have a lot of questions. I want to clarify that when I kissed you, I hadn't seen Teddy's father for about two months. I didn't even know I was pregnant. I'd only dated him for a few months before that."

"You don't owe me an explanation, Tish." Although I had plenty of curiosity about the situation, I meant what I said.

She leaned back, her fingertips tracing along the edge of the counter. "I want to explain." Her shoulders rose as she sucked in a deep breath. "Like I said, I'd only been dating him for a few months. We only had sex one time." Her cheeks flushed a deep shade of pink. "I can't believe I'm even telling you this, but he stealthed me."

"Stealth? Excuse me?" I prompted.

I could see her jaw tighten. "He took the condom off while we were having sex. He was so fast, I didn't even notice. I confronted him on the spot when I realized what had happened. That was the last time we talked. I've never been too regular, so I got a little worried when I missed my period, but I didn't panic right away." She swallowed audibly. "I can't even believe I'm telling you all this."

Anger crashed through me in an abrupt, unexpected wave. "What the fuck? What an asshole. Not you, him."

Tish rolled her eyes. "I was furious too. Even though I didn't plan any of this, I decided I wanted to keep the baby. Paul— That's Teddy's sperm donor," she clarified. "He hasn't responded to me since. I did text him that I was pregnant. I don't even want him to be involved. I figure I'll probably never hear from him again. He's a commercial fisherman."

"Fucking asshole," I muttered.

Her lips curled in a wry smile. "I appreciate your anger on my behalf. Anyway, that's what happened after we kissed. I found out I was pregnant. When Rhys asked me to write the posting for the job here, I realized it was a great opportunity for me, with better pay, and so on. With everything that happened, I kind of wanted the fresh start." She looked at me uncertainly.

"It all makes sense. So, how *are* you?" I repeated my earlier question.

Tish stared at me and let out a wondering laugh. "I'm great some days, I'm exhausted other days. Every minute of sleep I get is like pure gold. Teddy's five months now. He recently started sleeping up to six hours a night, which is fucking amazing. I went back to the office today. I thought I might freak out and run to the daycare and get him, but I didn't. I've been really lucky. Rhys helped a lot when I moved. He connected me with your brother Chase and your cousin Archer. I stayed in the garage apartment at Archer and Phoebe's place for a month. Through Phoebe, I met Madison and Graham. They rent this house, so when the last tenant moved out, Madison let me know. It has more space than the garage apartment, so I jumped on it."

"I'm staying in that same apartment right now. This is definitely a better fit with a baby," I offered.

She smiled back at me as she nodded. "So, here I am. I was kind of surprised you even wanted to see me. I thought maybe you would assume, I don't know, that I was seeing somebody else when we kissed."

"It's okay, Tish. You were worried about getting involved with me because you worked for my brother anyway."

"It's not like Rhys is the boss of my life. He was my boss," she corrected. "And I guess he's still my boss, but it's more distant now. I just worried it would be awkward."

"Maybe." I shrugged, trying to ignore the thrum of my heartbeat.

She laced her fingers together, twisting them nervously. I reached across the counter, catching her wrist in mine before I slid my hand down to curl around one of hers. "What are you so nervous about?"

She easily curled her hand into mine. "I don't know. Life has been a lot. You keep showing up when I never expect it."

I took a slow breath as my heart kicked along hard and fast and true. There was something about Tish for me, something startlingly true. I gathered my courage.

"I think what I'm about to say might scare you away, but I feel like I should say it anyway," I began.

"I don't scare easy," Tish said. "And, I'm sitting down, so I'm not likely to faint on you."

I chuckled. "Well, that's good. I don't know how to explain this, but I feel like something is supposed to happen between us. I've felt that since the first time we met."

"When you saved me from face-planting on the gravel?" she teased softly.

All I could do was nod. Quiet fell between us. I could hear the sound of a clock on the wall ticking and my heart echoing in rushing beats.

Eventually, she tipped her head to the side. "Maybe

so, but I have a baby. Having a baby is… Well, really, most of it is just a lot of work." She paused, letting out a soft sigh. "My life is a mess these days."

I didn't know what the hell had come over me. Every time I thought about Tish, I recalled the very first time we met when she fainted. I didn't even know what I wanted. I just wanted, for once, to have a chance with her not to slip through my fingers.

"I get that. Let me clarify. First, I met you and you fainted. When I asked for your number, you said maybe you'd give it to me if we saw each other ever again." Her lips twisted to the side and she rolled her eyes a little. "Imagine my surprise when I saw you at my brother's wedding and came to find out you were Rhys's assistant. I might've known that sooner, except I didn't go to the office much and I didn't live in Fireweed Harbor." I pressed my tongue in my cheek as I considered my words. "And, now you're here."

"So are you," she said softly.

"Before you go thinking I'm some kind of creep and followed you here, they decided to relocate the whole hotshot crew here. It was either move here, or make a career decision. At some point, I will work for my family's company, but not yet. It turns out what they want me to do is handle the brewery here in Willow Brook when it's up and running. I won't pretend I didn't think about you and didn't wonder about you, but I promise I didn't chase you here."

She squeezed my hand. "I know. You're not that kind of guy."

"You trust me that much?" I teased lightly.

She lifted one shoulder in a small shrug. "I guess I do. I trust Rhys and he trusts you. But more than that, it's a feeling."

Just then, there was the distinct sound of a

stomach growling. Tish's cheeks flushed a delightful shade of pink. "That's me. I forget to eat a lot. Babies do that to a person."

"I won't pretend I have a big repertoire in the kitchen, but I'm a solid cook. I can whip up some dinner if you have anything for me to work with."

"These days, I pretty much live off anything I can put in the microwave. I don't have a lot of options." She cast a sheepish smile at that.

I gave her hand a quick squeeze before reluctantly releasing it to stand. "Can I see what our options are?"

Her laugh was a dry rustle before she waved a hand in an arc. "Go for it. I literally have nothing to hide. I'm too tired to be embarrassed about the state of my kitchen."

A quick glance through her cabinets and refrigerator revealed that she liked macaroni and cheese and she had a few frozen meals. Otherwise, the pickings were slim.

Resting my hips against the counter, I curled my hands on the edge. "The situation calls for macaroni and cheese. I'll make it fancy."

Tish giggled. I was pretty sure it was the first time I'd heard her giggle. The sound was like a little lasso, catching my heart and cinching tight.

"You're going to make me some macaroni and cheese?" Her brows rose as a smile played at the corners of her mouth.

"Absolutely. It's not just for you. I'm always hungry, and I love mac and cheese."

"I can help," she said.

I held a hand up. "Nope. I'm on it. There's a baby asleep and you are going to sit right there and not worry about dinner. Just tell me where everything is."

Knowing from Rhys that Tish was very much a doer kind of person, it said something about how tired she was that she really did let me take over. She showed me where the saucepan was and filled it with water. When I redirected her to sit down, she did.

She didn't have anything to drink other than water. In short order, I had made a double batch of mac and cheese from boxes and added tons of extra cheese, along with a dash of chipotle seasoning.

A few bites in, Tish smiled over at me. "Thank you. This is absolutely delicious."

After we finished eating, I refused to let her clean up, although she nudged me out of the way and insisted on putting the dishes in the dishwasher after I rinsed them.

"You're here in Willow Brook for real?" she prompted at one point.

"For real. I go by the station to pick up the HR paperwork tomorrow. I still work for the state, but it's a new location so that means new forms. That's always fun," I said.

"Paperwork is totally my jam," she said solemnly.

I burst out laughing. "It is, isn't it?"

Her eyes crinkled with her smile as she shrugged. "It is." She looked toward the clock mounted on the wall above the stove.

"Am I overstaying my welcome?"

She shook her head quickly. "No! It's actually nice to have an adult in the house. Don't get me wrong, I love Teddy. Even though I didn't plan any of this, I'm pretty sure he's the best thing that ever happened to me. I have mixed feelings about it, but I'm really ready to be back at work. Being home all the time with a baby, mostly by myself, is not really a life I want. I feel kind of alone a lot."

"Just tell me when to leave. We can hang out here

in the kitchen and you can talk about whatever you want. Or we could watch a show? Your call."

She had one hand curled on the edge of the counter, and the other was spinning her hair around her fingers. At some point, while she was eating, her ponytail had fallen. Her silky brown hair was in a messy tousle around her shoulders.

I was standing across from her, leaning against the counter beside the sink. There were maybe two feet between us. Her eyes were soft as she looked at me. In a fiery second, she stunned the hell out of me by pushing away from the counter and taking two steps to stand immediately in front of me.

"We have unfinished business," she announced.

When her palm landed on my chest, it was as if she had slapped a magnet against it. My heart was the opposing force, yanked suddenly forward toward her touch.

This woman muddled my thoughts and grabbed any semblance of control straight out of my hands. I scrambled to think. "We do?"

"Yes, firefighter, we do. I've been thinking about it since you mentioned earlier that it felt like there was something there for us."

"You've been thinking this whole time?" My brows hitched up.

A delightful pink flush rose on her cheeks again as she smiled with the tiniest hint of bashfulness in it. "I have. You kissed me, and it feels like another planet, another timeline entirely because so much has happened in my life since then — babies will do that. That night, after you left, I had seriously mixed feelings because I wanted a lot more than a kiss. I had wished that I didn't work for your brother. Not that he has a say, but it's your family's company, and..." She shrugged.

"I get that part. Could be awkward for you." She seemed a little surprised at my easy acceptance of that. "I don't like it," I added. "But it is what it is."

"It is, but it's different now. I don't work directly for Rhys."

She moved just a little closer and her soft curves pressed against me. "Maybe it's been too long for me to ask if we can pick up where we left off?"

When her eyes darkened and she slid her tongue across her bottom lip, there was no way in any universe I could've done anything other than kiss her. I slid an arm around her waist and dipped my head. The need slicing through me was so sharp it was almost painful. Yet, I wanted to savor this moment. My forehead fell to hers, and I forced myself to take a slow breath.

She smelled a little sweet and salty. I brushed my lips over hers again, intending to take this slow. Tish was having none of that. She made this little raspy sound in the back of her throat before she arched up and curled her hand around the back of my neck to pull me closer. When her lips opened underneath mine, I was gone.

When she arched closer against me, and I felt the taut little peaks of her nipples through the thin cotton of my T-shirt, I let out a ragged groan. On the heels of a gulp of air when we briefly broke apart, I tightened my arm around her waist and slid my hand into her hair as I angled her head to the side and claimed her mouth.

Chapter Sixteen

TISH

When I felt the subtle sting on my scalp from Griffin's fingers gripping my hair as he took over our kiss, I thought I might burst into flames. I needed this — *him* — so desperately. It was a bone-deep craving.

I felt as if I could lose myself in his kiss, and I wanted to. Maybe it was the memory of our first kiss, which felt like another time and place, almost as if it had happened to another person. Except there was a kernel in it that brought it back to me. Our kiss went on and on and on. One of my hands slid down his back. I could feel the strength of him, his corded muscles flexing under my touch. My hand crept under the hem of his T-shirt, greedy to feel him.

His skin was hot to the touch, and I savored his warmth and strength. I gasped into his mouth when his hand slid through my hair and down my back, boldly cupping my bottom and pressing me closer. I could feel his hard length against my lower belly. Seconds later, we broke apart and the sound of our ragged breathing filled the air around us.

His eyes bored into mine. "I think we need to slow down."

I was shaking my head before I could even think it through. I didn't want to slow down. I wanted to dive into this fire and let it consume me.

The whole experience of pregnancy and giving birth had been messy, exhausting, and painful. None of it was sexy, and yet all of it brought you into your body in a way that, at least, for me, not much else could. In the aftermath of trying to find a rhythm amidst the chaos of sleepless nights and nursing and being entirely responsible for a tiny human, my barriers had fallen away, and had stripped me raw. Now, I simply wanted what I wanted.

In this moment, that was Griffin. I slid my palm over his abs and down over the hot length of him.

"Tish," he bit out through gritted teeth.

I leaned back slightly, lifting my chin. "I want this. I want you."

He swallowed. "If you want me to stop, I will. We don't have to do anything more than kiss."

Griffin seemed to have some sort of misplaced idea that we should stop with just a kiss. Whatever. I was well beyond that. I narrowed my eyes. "I don't want just a kiss."

After a weighted moment, he dipped his head again, claiming my mouth once more. His kiss was a little slower, lingering this time. I dragged my palm up and down his length, and he groaned into my mouth. Impatient, I quickly unbuttoned his jeans and slid his zipper down before slipping my hand into the opening.

I savored the little thrill that zipped through me when his cock pulsed under my touch. I wasn't usually this bold, but I felt caught in a rushing current. I broke away from his mouth before shoving his jeans down, just far enough to free his cock. I curled my palm around him, watching his eyes darken, his chest rising and falling with his rapid breathing.

"Is this okay? Do you want me to stop?" I whispered.

"Fuck, no! Don't stop," he gasped.

Kneeling down, I brought my mouth to the tip of his cock, licking the drop of cum rolling out.

"Fuck, Tish," he murmured, his fingers gripping my hair.

I kept my eyes on his as I angled my head to the side and circled my tongue around his thick crown. My gaze finally broke away from his when I shifted to take him into my mouth fully. Curling my palm around the base of his shaft, I teased him with deep suction and slid my tongue along the underside of his cock. I savored the earthy tang.

"Tish," he bit out.

I released him with a little pop before asking, "Yes?"

This encounter had spiraled completely out of my control. My release was *right* there.

Staring down at Tish, it felt as if lightning was reverberating through me in jagged bolts of heat. Her lips were swollen and damp from the magic she had wrought on my cock over the last few moments.

I tried to answer, but as the moment stretched, she slid her palm up and down my cock before leaning forward to suck me into her mouth again. That was it. The tether of my control snapped, and my release spurted into her mouth.

Thank fuck there was a counter behind me, because otherwise my knees would've given out. I was still trying to gather myself together when she straightened and stepped to the sink to rinse out her mouth.

A moment later, she stood in front of me, looking pleased and sexy as hell.

I studied her for a few beats before reaching out and hooking my finger over the waistband of her cotton pants. "Come here." I gave her a small tug.

She didn't hesitate. I almost groaned when I felt the soft curves of her breasts against my chest. "Well." I lifted my hand to brush her hair away from her face. "You took me off guard there."

Her smile was sly. "I kind of wanted to."

"You did?"

She bit the corner of her lip, still smiling as she looked up at me. "Yeah. The first two times I saw you, I fainted. You've usually had the upper hand with me."

I chuckled. Need was still revving its engine in my body, and Tish was feathering the pedal.

I couldn't help it. I *had* to kiss her again. Everything felt out of order, and yet that seemed to be how it went with Tish.

I savored the soft sounds that she made at the back of her throat, the way her tongue glided against mine. I took deep sips from her, breathing her in. Having already found my release had given me some control. I wasn't so rushed, the claws of need weren't so sharp now. I let my hands explore her—the dip of her waist, the way her hips flared out, the softness of her bottom when I gave her a squeeze.

She broke away abruptly and leaned back. "Just so you know, I had a baby."

"Um, I know. Why are you saying this now?"

For the first time tonight, hesitation flickered in her gaze and she looked a little bashful. She cleared her throat. "Um, things are, well, curvier."

"I like you just the way you are."

I claimed her mouth in another deep kiss and let my hands slide up under her shirt. Her skin was warm and silky. I slid my palm around her waist, up over the curve of her belly to one of her breasts.

They were plump and full, her nipples pebbled peaks.

She let out a little whimper, arching into my palm. I deftly unbuttoned her shirt with my free hand until it draped open. I dipped my head down, nipping along the side of her neck, savoring the way she arched against me. I felt the goosebumps rise on her skin and teased my thumbs over her nipples.

Her fingers speared into my hair and she let out a sharp cry as I dallied with lazy kisses along her collarbone. I was lost in the sounds she made, her sweet, musky scent, and the softness of her skin. When I lifted my head, she let out a frustrated sigh. "Don't stop."

"Just rearranging," I said as I spun us around.

I'd recovered from my release and was steady on my feet again. I turned her around and lifted her hips onto the counter, pausing for a moment to take her in. Her hair was a messy tousle around her shoulders, her cheeks were flushed deep pink. With her shirt open and her breasts exposed, she looked elementally feminine and sultry. It felt as if a cord was connected between us, shimmering with fire.

Her knees were open slightly, and I stepped between them as I cupped a breast, sliding my thumb back and forth over her nipple. I smoothed a palm over the curve of her belly, delving between her thighs and cupping her mound to discover her panties were soaked from her arousal.

Her lips were parted as she stared at me, her breath coming in sharp pants.

"Sweetness, I'm gonna make you come," I rasped.

She stared at me, her eyes darkening. "Please."

I slid my arm around her waist, splaying it at the base of her spine as I pulled her a little closer to the edge of the counter. Her hips shifted toward me slightly. She let out a whimper before I gave in and pushed her panties out of the way to delve into her slippery wet folds.

I held her gaze when I sank two fingers, knuckle-deep, into her.

"Please, hurry," she gasped.

"Tell me what you need, sweetness."

I could barely think through the fiery haze. "Make me come. Please. Now..." was all I could manage.

Griffin pumped his fingers into me deeply, barely grazing over my clit. I was desperate, I could hardly bear the pressure tightening inside. Again and again, he sank his fingers into me, stretching me and pushing me closer and closer to the edge. My hips were rocking into his touch.

"Griffin, now, please!" I demanded.

He pumped in deeply, his thumb working magic over my clit. My orgasm hit me so hard and fast that I barely heard myself crying his name in a ragged breath as my release slammed through me. Sensation drew tight before breaking apart with such force I trembled all over. I was grateful for his arm around my waist to hold me as my head fell to the curve of his neck.

I stayed like that for a long moment. The pleasure slowed to small waves and eddies before he withdrew his fingers and tucked my panties back into place. I breathed, barely pulling myself together.

Eventually, I lifted my head. He was right there

waiting and dipped his head to give me a kiss. I didn't know if it was months of exhaustion with a baby, or the tension I'd been functioning under, or just the fact that *finally* this happened with Griffin, but I felt more relaxed than I could ever remember feeling. I was sated on a deep level, down to my bones. I felt liquid and languid.

When Griffin drew back and lifted a hand to smooth my messy hair away from my forehead, it felt as if shimmering threads were catching between us and tightening. Although this felt undeniably right, I wasn't prepared to examine that feeling. I desperately didn't want him to leave yet.

A few minutes later, I was sitting on the small couch in the living room. Griffin's gaze arced about the space. The living room had windows offering a view of a field and trees. With it being late summer, the fireweed blooms were falling, leaving faded fuchsia flowers scattered over the ground. The last rays of the sun still angled over the mountains.

There was a stone fireplace to one side and bookshelves lining the other wall. An archway led to the kitchen with a hallway on the opposite side where the bedrooms were.

"This is a nice place," he said, catching my eyes.

"It is. I'm grateful that Madison and Graham rented it to me."

"I'm glad it was available. It's the perfect size for you and Teddy."

"Thank you for making me dinner," I said after a pause.

"I made mac and cheese. Nothing amazing," he pointed out.

I bit my lip to keep from smiling too much. "I know, but I happen to love mac and cheese. I'm sure you could guess that based on the state of my kitchen cabinets. I have help from friends, but it's a lot to have a baby by yourself."

I didn't realize how battened down I'd been keeping myself until the emotion rushed up and I felt tears stinging my eyes. I wasn't sad that I had a baby. Teddy was the best thing that had ever happened to me. But it felt like I was constantly spinning plates in the air just to get by. I was overwhelmed with the idea of trying to go back to work and still do everything I needed to do.

Griffin slid across the short distance between us on the couch and curled his strong arm around my shoulders. His touch was warm and reassuring and solid, everything I needed.

"Of course, it's a lot. No need to explain. I will make mac and cheese any night you want it."

I didn't want to move away, so I shifted slightly to lean back and look at him. "You mean that, don't you?"

He didn't miss a beat. "Absolutely." He paused, studying me. "Now, we have to do the awkward thing."

"What's the awkward thing?" I asked.

"You'll probably find a way to kick me out politely."

"What if I don't want you to leave?"

Chapter Nineteen

GRIFFIN

My brain felt hazy the following morning. After our intensely intimate encounter and Tish asking me to stay, we fell asleep in her bedroom. Teddy woke up once during the night, and Tish had tried to shoo me away, but I sat up against the pillows with her while she nursed for a few minutes before he fell back asleep.

In the morning, she seemed to start gathering up her doubts again. She had to go to work, and it was obvious her mornings were a rush. She was still trying to settle into a new routine. Despite the hurry, I'd gotten a kiss. When our lips were barely touching as I lifted my head, I whispered, "It was really, *really*, good to see you, Tish.

In that tiny pocket of time, it felt as if it was just us in the world. Her lips curled into a smile and the guarded look in her eyes had fallen away. "It was really good to see you, too, Griffin."

Teddy let out a little squawk. He was already in his car seat, ready to be carted to the car. In the following few minutes, Tish's hands were full with an array of baby things, a diaper bag, and more.

I eyed her. "I can carry Teddy, or everything else."

For a split second, she hesitated before laughing softly. "If you don't mind, you can take him. He's the heaviest."

After Teddy was secured in the back of her car, I reluctantly left. A short drive later, I walked into Firehouse Café.

"Well, you look a little tired, Griffin," Janet observed from behind the counter.

"Do I?" I countered.

Her brows hitched up. "You do, but some coffee might help. What can I get you?"

"Since I *am* a little tired, how about a really strong coffee? I'm not a complicated man. Your house coffee will do, if it's strong enough."

"Oh, it's strong, but I'll add a shot of espresso for you. That'll make it even stronger."

While I waited, I glanced around. The place was bustling. With most of the tables filled, and what seemed like an endless line of customers coming through the door.

I was still waiting for my coffee when I heard my name. Glancing over, I saw Beck.

"Hey," Beck said, stepping out of the line to clap me on the shoulder. "Are you getting food or just coffee?"

"I started with coffee," I replied.

"Dude, you have to get one of her sandwiches. She has a secret special." He wagged his brows dramatically with that.

When I glanced toward Janet as she handed me my coffee, she rolled her eyes. "It's not a secret. Beck likes to pretend like it is."

"It's a secret until I get it for him," Beck countered with a grin.

Janet chuckled.

"You don't have to get me breakfast," I replied.

"He's going to insist," Maisie piped up at his side.

"Go for it. I'll return the favor another time," I said with a shrug.

Sandwich in hand, I walked out with them. "You headed to the station?" Beck asked as I stopped beside my truck. At my nod, he added, "Perfect. We'll eat there."

Only minutes later, I was sitting in the kitchen at the station, enjoying the excellent breakfast sandwich Beck had gotten for me. Maisie had kissed him on the cheek and headed out front.

He smiled over at me after he finished a bite. "Marriage is the best."

"Is it now?" I returned.

Graham chuckled as he approached the table. "Beck is all about marriage. It's funny. In high school, he was the biggest flirt ever."

"Legendary," Cade Masters quipped, as he stopped beside Graham.

Beck was unruffled. "I've got two kids, and I adore my wife and it's just good. Are you married?"

Graham snorted as he sat down in a chair beside me, clapping me on the shoulder. "Buckle up. Beck is the station gossip. Nosy as fuck."

Once again, Beck shrugged. "I like information. I don't spread gossip. I just gather gossip."

A laugh sputtered up as I looked over at him. "I guess I know who to go to if I have a question about something."

"Well, first, answer mine," Beck teased.

"I'm not married. Dating doesn't work out that well as a hotshot firefighter."

Beck shook his head vigorously. "Now, see that's where you're wrong. Graham's happily married, I'm happily married, so is Cade."

Cade rolled his eyes as he patted Beck on the shoulder and kept walking.

"Good to know." I finished off my sandwich and took a swallow of coffee. "That's some damn good coffee." I lowered the cup to the table, studying the distinctive red cup with Firehouse Café emblazoned on the side.

Beck was still on the topic of marriage. "You just need to find the right person."

"Are you giving me dating advice now?" I asked.

Graham laughed at my side. "He most certainly is."

My thoughts spun back to Tish and our startlingly intimate encounter last night. I didn't need to find the right woman, but I could definitely use some advice. Not yet though.

"I guess I know who to go to when I need that," I finally said.

Beck grinned widely. "I'm your guy."

I let out a wondering laugh. "He always like this?" I addressed Graham.

"Usually. All joking aside, Beck's as good as they come, and his advice is usually spot on. I don't like admitting it, but I will."

Beck was beaming when I looked over at him again. After that, Graham took me around and introduced me to a few others in the station, lastly taking me out front to introduce me again to Maisie. She promptly handed me a sheaf of paperwork. "I know you already worked for the state up in Fairbanks, and in Fireweed Harbor, but —"

I cut in, "New location, new documentation. No need to apologize."

Maisie's dimples appeared with her smile. "I like you," she announced. "You don't have to do it all right now. You can take it home. Just get it to me by next week."

I texted Tish to check in during the day. I could practically feel her blush through her text when I told her the night before had been incredible. Despite my impatience, I knew I needed to put the ball firmly in her court. The depth of my feelings for her wasn't logical by any stretch. They never had been, all the way back to when we first met on the side of the highway.

I forced myself to focus on work. Although we weren't out fighting fires, there was plenty to focus on with meeting various people at the station and getting the lay of the land. I told myself I would go ahead and deal with the pesky HR paperwork. I knew it would take me longer than most.

I was just sitting down at the break table in the kitchen area when Graham plunked down in a chair across from me, resting his elbows on the table. "So, we have a few positions to fill. I'm assuming you want to be part of the interviews."

I glanced up. As one of the leads on the crew, this was part of the deal. "I'd love to, if I'm not stepping on anyone's toes."

"Nope. It's you and me leading the crew. I want your take. I asked Maisie to shuffle through the applications. As I'm sure you know, there's a shortage of wildland firefighters. Although, lots of people like coming to Alaska. Should I tell her to set up a few interviews for us?"

"Go for it. My schedule is open until we head out into the field, which you know."

Graham flashed a grin before tipping his head to the side. "I like you."

"That's a good thing, seeing as we're going to spend a lot of time together."

Graham clapped me on the shoulder as he stood from the table. Beck was approaching from the hallway. "Before you know it, Beck'll be trying to set you up with somebody."

"Aside from being nosy, he's a matchmaker?" I teased.

Jonah came out of the hallway, pausing by the table. I'd met him about an hour prior after he finished working out. "Oh, he is," he replied with a snort.

"He can focus on somebody other than me. What about you?"

Jonah rolled his eyes. "Already married. Love her."

Beck's cell phone rang. "Oh, shit." He glanced at the screen. "I gotta roll. Picking up one of the kids from daycare, and I almost spaced it."

With a few other firefighters pausing to greet me, I decided to ignore my paperwork for now. Hours later, as I was leaving, Tish's name flashed on my screen. Hope jolted me.

Tish: *Something came up at work. I hate to impose, but I'm wondering if you could pick up Teddy from daycare for me. I can call over and let them know you'll be picking him up. I wouldn't ask, except I can't leave yet. Somebody got injured over at the construction site and I'm dealing with the follow-up. Should be done in about an hour or two.*

Me: *Of course. Tell me where to go and make sure to give them my full name.*

I hustled out to my truck and hopped in, glancing down to see her reply.

Tish: *You're a godsend. I've already called the daycare. I really, really, really appreciate it. His car seat is at the daycare. The house is unlocked. I'll see you there.*

Me: *I'll see you when you get home. Don't worry about the time.*

Tish thanked me again, and texted me the address of the daycare. When I arrived to pick up Teddy, the woman at the front eyed me suspiciously. "We'll need to see ID."

I handed it over. Once I had Teddy and all of his things, the woman stifled a laugh when she saw me juggling him in his car seat and the diaper bag. I grinned over at her. "I'm getting there."

It felt strange to have a baby in the back when I began driving. He didn't fuss at all and giggled after I got him situated. I had to review the instructions to make sure I buckled the car seat in properly. Although I was an uncle to several nieces and nephews, being solely responsible like this carried an unexpected weight.

Chapter Twenty

GRIFFIN

I discovered when I got back to Tish's house that being responsible for a baby also meant I didn't check my phone very much. I had multiple texts from Tish. It was clear she was sending them via talk-to-text because there were some amusing errors. She sent me tips on feeding and more.

We got through dinner, which was messier than I expected, and he still hadn't fussed very much. I changed his diaper and was startled when there was a knock at the door. Confused, I scooped him back up and he started mouthing his fist. I opened the door to find Graham there.

"Griffin?" His eyes widened.

"Graham, what are you doing here?"

"Well Tish rents this place from us and I saw an unfamiliar vehicle here so I stopped by to make sure everything was okay."

"Who is it?" a voice came from behind him.

Madison appeared, along with a young woman. "Who are you?" she demanded.

Graham gestured to her. "This is my daughter,

Allie. She babysits for Tish a lot. We were coming home from picking her up at the airport in Anchorage."

Teddy recognized Allie and began to babble excitedly. I handed him over because I thought Allie might be upset if I didn't.

"You know Tish?" Madison asked.

"She works for my family's company," I explained.

"Oh, right." Madison nodded.

Allie was still looking a little suspicious about the whole thing. I held my hands up. "You can call Tish right now. She texted me because she had to stay late at work to deal with something."

Graham chuckled. "I should've recognized your truck."

Allie bounced Teddy in her arms as he giggled. "I can take him if you want," she offered.

"I promised Tish I'd stay with him, so I probably should."

Graham smiled at her. "Griffin can handle Teddy."

Allie reluctantly handed the baby back to me, adding, "If he has trouble falling asleep, text me."

"Thanks for checking on Tish," I said.

Madison smiled up at Graham. "The first time I met Graham, he thought I was breaking and entering in the house where we live now."

His gaze arced toward the trees. "We're right through there. I take care of my neighbors."

"I appreciate it. Good neighbors are good to have," I replied.

After they left, Teddy settled quickly when I sat down on the couch with him. It was only minutes after Graham, Madison, and Allie had left that Tish arrived home.

"Hey!" she called when she came through the door.

I scooped Teddy into my arms and walked into the entry area to greet her. Teddy began kicking his feet against my thighs and bouncing, overjoyed to see his mom.

"Somebody's happy to see you," I teased lightly.

Tish dropped her purse on the floor and immediately took him from me, kissing him on both cheeks and smoothing his hair.

I picked up her purse and set it on a nearby table.

"Thank you so much," she said.

My heart gave a tricky beat in my chest as I smiled over at her. "Anytime."

She kicked off her shoes, still holding Teddy in her arms, and followed me into the kitchen.

She grinned over at me. "You got food."

"I picked up takeout on the way over. Before you think I'm amazing, Maisie recommended this gallery café. I'm not sure if you've eaten there yet."

Teddy was tiring quickly. His head had fallen onto her shoulder. While I wasn't a baby expert, I spent enough time with my nieces and nephews to know that it was downright remarkable how a baby could go from wide awake to sound asleep in a matter of minutes.

"I've eaten there once or twice. Good call. What did they have tonight?" Tish asked.

"Tonight was American southern food specialties. To be honest, it sounds amazing and I've had to be patient for you to get here."

Tish giggled, and my heart flipped in my chest. The effect she had on me was shockingly powerful. She glanced down at her shoulder. "Let me go put him in his crib."

"The woman at the daycare said he was good today.

Some naps and playtime. She said he's an easy baby," I offered.

"Honestly, that's what everyone tells me. He's my only baby, but he seems pretty easygoing."

Tish walked out of the kitchen with Teddy. "I'll get some plates out for us if you don't mind me rummaging in your cabinets," I added.

"Rummage away. I'll be right back."

I could hear the soft murmur of her voice talking to him as she walked down the hallway. A few minutes later, she reappeared. "You changed Teddy's diaper."

"Uh, yeah. He needed a diaper change. Did you think I would leave him in a dirty diaper?"

She shrugged, looking a little sheepish. "I didn't know if you'd changed a diaper before."

"You know Rhys has little Jake, and maybe you're not up to speed on the rest of the family, but I have other babies in my life. I wouldn't claim to be a diaper expert, but I can do the task."

Tish stopped by the edge of the island, her eyes lingering on me for a moment. She looked down, her gaze arcing over the platter of food I'd set out along with two plates. A second later, she rounded the counter and stopped immediately in front of me before leaning up and pressing a soft kiss on the underside of my jaw. Her touch was hot and electrifying.

"Thank you," she said. "I feel like I say that to you a lot."

She stepped back, and I experienced a moment where it felt as if my entire body was leaning toward her.

"The first time you met me, I fainted," she continued. "You kept me from falling on my face, fetched me out of the harbor, and now you're babysitting on short notice."

As I held her gaze, the air around us came to life, shimmering with electricity. It wasn't simply a physical draw to her. There was something emotional threading through it.

I cleared my throat. "You don't need to thank me. It's my pleasure. I actually kind of like babies. They're cute and uncomplicated."

Tish burst out laughing. By the time she stopped, there were tears in her eyes.

"I wasn't trying to be funny," I pointed out.

She shrugged. "Maybe not, but I get your point. Babies are uncomplicated in some ways. I was laughing because the last year or so has been the most complicated time of my life. I feel like I kind of finally settled into something resembling sanity within the last month or so. Even though I'm glad to be back at work, I feel a little guilty."

The sound of her stomach growling interrupted us. I smiled at her. "Sit down and eat."

Chapter Twenty-One

GRIFFIN

"Oh, my God," Tish moaned in between bites. "This is so good."

I finished chewing before taking a swallow of water. "It is."

Upon Maisie's advice, I had gone with the variety option. In this case, that turned out to be collard greens with ham, which were freaking amazing, the cheesiest mashed potatoes I'd ever had in my life, crispy fried chicken, and fried okra.

"I hope they do this one more often," she said after she finished another bite of the cheesy potatoes.

"I would eat this every night," I said, meaning it.

Tish smiled over at me. She had filled me in on what happened at work. One of the construction workers had fallen and broken his arm. She had wanted to make sure all the loose ends were tied up before they left the hospital.

"I'm so grateful I could get a hold of you. Graham's daughter Allie, who's in college, helps out whenever she can, but she was out of town."

"Oh, that reminds me. Madison and Graham

stopped by with Allie on the way from picking her up at the airport. I think they thought I was breaking and entering. Apparently, that's how Graham and Madison met," I said with a chuckle.

"Oh, I've heard that story. Nice of them to stop by. Allie is awesome. They've been so helpful since I moved here. Thanks to Rhys giving me a few contacts when I moved here, I already have a really good support network."

"You can thank yourself. Rhys always said you were his best assistant. He wanted to support you taking this position."

"Either way, I appreciate his help. I think Rhys's new assistant is going to be great. He might be more efficient than me."

"Rhys is pretty happy so far. Haven assures me it's going well."

I eyed her for a few beats. "Are you glad you moved to Willow Brook?"

Chapter Twenty-Two

TISH

I set my fork down and took a swallow of water. "I am. It's been a big change, but then coming to Alaska was a big change. When the expansion position opened up, I wanted a chance to have more responsibility."

Unspoken was the fact I'd been pregnant when I moved. That truly wasn't the reason I left, but I found myself explaining anyway. Maybe I needed to say it aloud for myself, as much as to explain it to Griffin.

"Do you judge me? I shouldn't have kissed you that night. It makes it seem like I was dating two people. I hadn't seen or heard from him for almost two months at that point."

Griffin shook his head. "Stop worrying about that. We kissed once, and you made it clear that you were worried about the complications of working for my brother. I suppose I should ask how you feel about that now."

"Conflicted," I answered honestly. "Rhys isn't my direct boss here, but it's still your family's corporation."

"I don't work there though."

"But you will at some point. Isn't the plan for you to take over at the brewery?" I asked.

"Someday." Griffin hesitated, his gaze considering. "After last night, I'm gonna need you to tell me now if it's a problem."

"If what's a problem?" I hedged. My heartbeat reverberated like a drum. I felt breathless and filled with sparks

"Us being involved. I like you, Tish. A lot. Way back when we first met, you said if we saw each other again, maybe that would be a sign."

Hope shot up little flares up inside, but I forced myself to be practical. "I know, but that was before I had a baby. My life is kind of complicated and messy now."

"Not to me," he said.

I swallowed, feeling my lips curl up. "Okay. I'll probably worry if things don't go well, but I guess I'm feeling selfish. I like you."

Griffin's smile was wide when he leaned across and gave me a quick kiss before standing and starting to pick up our plates.

I leapt up. "You don't have to clean up! You made dinner for me the other night –"

"Mac and cheese from a box," he pointed out dryly.

"I know, but –"

I had reached the counter beside him now. He rested his hands on my hips and looked down in my eyes. "Tish, you had a long day. I'm just gonna rinse the plates and put them in the dishwasher. Not a hardship."

I bit my lip. "Okay," I whispered. "I'll put the leftovers away."

Griffin had ordered a lot of food, enough to feed a big family. When I pointed out as much as I was putting the food away, he glanced over. "That was on purpose. You're a busy mom. I figure some leftovers might be handy to have around."

My belly felt funny and my heart flipped over in my chest as I stared at this man. He made me weak in the knees and made me want things that were absolutely crazy.

After we finished tidying up the kitchen, I checked on Teddy. He was sound asleep. I adjusted the volume on the baby monitor and set the remote on the coffee table before plunking down on the couch. Rolling my head to the side, I glanced over toward Griffin. "Are you staying or going?"

His gaze was warm as he walked with deliberate strides to stop in front of me. "I was hoping you would ask me to stay."

I was tired. Honestly, I'd been tired since I had Teddy. And yet, the effect Griffin had on me was something wild. When I looked up and saw the banked embers flickering in the depths of his eyes, my body responded with heat pooling low in my belly and a shivery sense of anticipation prickling over my skin.

I patted the couch beside me. I was trying to play it cool, but I could barely contain myself. When he sat down beside me, I told myself we would turn on the TV and I would behave like a regular person where there was a baby asleep in the other room. Instead, I wanted to climb him like a tree. When I looked over and found his gaze waiting, I couldn't help myself. Impulsively, I leaned over and kissed him on the cheek.

When I began to draw back, he reached for me, cupping my nape and whispering, "Let me kiss you, sweetness."

My entire body swooned and my ovaries did a little

dance, jumping up and down in excitement for more of Griffin and the magic he wrought with my body.

"Okay," I whispered against his lips just before he gave me a lingering kiss.

By the time we broke apart, I could barely breathe and I was near desperate for him. I shifted my legs, restless for more. We stared at each other and I was a little relieved to discover his breath was ragged like mine.

"Fuck, Tish," he muttered. His head fell back against the couch.

"Let's..." I scrambled onto his lap, straddling him.

He lifted his head, and his dark, intent gaze snagged mine. "Let's what?" he prompted.

I felt suddenly bashful. I wasn't usually this direct. Yet Griffin had this effect on me where I forgot to be self-conscious, where I forgot to feel insecure.

He rocked his hips slightly and I let out a startled moan. I hadn't planned it that way, because I wasn't planning any of this, but I had landed with his cock nestled against my core.

"Well, you said fuck," I finally murmured. "I was thinking we could do that."

The word seemed a little dirty, but Griffin called to all of the elemental parts of me, including my heart.

His eyes held mine, ensnaring me in the electric heat of his gaze. "Are you sure?" he asked, lightly cupping my cheek and tracing his thumb along the line of my cheekbone to my bottom lip.

I swallowed. "Yes," I rasped.

There was a long moment that stretched like an elastic band between us before his hand fell away from my cheek. He gripped me by the hips and rocked into me. "Whatever you want. I mean that."

"I know you do," I said between ragged gasps.

"Do you want me to stay tonight?"

I swallowed and nodded. Seconds later, we were tumbling from one kiss into the next. I could barely breathe as my pulse rushed through my body. At some point, I broke away.

I didn't even know what I needed other than— everything, all of him.

He lifted me off his lap and stood. "You're wearing too many clothes," I managed to say.

His chuckle sent goosebumps rising in a prickle all over.

"We're in agreement on that." His fingers began to unbutton my blouse.

For the first time in months, I'd worn something other than what I'd thrown on when I woke up, which was usually sweatpants and a T-shirt. I'd worn a blouse and slacks. Maybe dressier than necessary for work-casual in Alaska, but I'd wanted the change of pace.

His actions galvanized me, and I shoved his T-shirt up his chest. He gave me a little assist, lifting it up over his head in a quick swoop while I unbuttoned his jeans.

It was practically a race at that point as we yanked at each other's clothes. My blouse fell to the floor and I shimmied out of my slacks, hooking my hands over my panties at the same time.

Griffin chuckled, murmuring, "You *are* efficient, Tish."

"I'm all about being efficient," I teased.

I felt the surface of his palm as he slid it up my belly to hook his thumb under the clasp of my bra and snap it loose. I shoved his boxers down, and he was reaching for me as he sat back down on the couch. Just as I moved to straddle him, he held me still.

"Wait." His voice was ragged.

"For what?"

"A condom," he nearly choked out.

He reached around me to where his jeans had fallen on the edge of the couch and fished out his wallet and then a condom. I wanted to dispute the point and tell him I had an IUD now. Because, holy hell, even though I adored Teddy, I would never again rely on condoms for birth control.

A moment later, Griffin was rolling the condom on, his eyes on mine the whole time as he protected us both.

His hands fell to my hips. "You could still change your mind, you know," he said.

"If you make me wait any longer..." I warned.

The fire in his eyes sizzled as he shifted and reached between us. I rose up when he positioned his thick crown at my entrance. Locked in his gaze, I could barely breathe at the feel of him filling me in a slow, slick slide. He seated himself fully with a subtle thrust of his hips upward.

"Oh, sweetness," he murmured. He gripped my hips, holding me in place when I began to move restlessly. "Give me a minute."

The moment was intense, a tangle of intimacy, fierce passion, and an almost primal sense of need spiraling through me. He leaned forward, catching my lips in a slow, sensual kiss. When he drew back, he rocked his hips upward. Everything began to speed up, one wave rolling into the next. The pleasure began to tighten like a knot inside of me, clenching at my core. Little pings of pleasure radiated outward from the friction created where we were joined.

I gasped, biting my lip, as I felt myself teetering on the edge.

"Oh, Tish..." Griffin released one of my hips and

reached between us to tease his fingers over my slippery, swollen clit.

He gave me just enough pressure to topple me over that edge I was racing toward. Everything pulled tight to an almost unbearable pressure before snapping free. I shattered inside, the waves crashing through me as I cried his name.

I felt his fingers pressing on my hips as he filled me once more. On the heels of a deep thrust, he threw his head back and shuddered with me. He cried my name in a gruff shout.

My own climax was ricocheting through me as we trembled together. The force of it slowed.

He banded one arm around my waist as I curled into him. We breathed together, and I savored the feel of his heartbeat pounding against mine.

Chapter Twenty-Three

GRIFFIN

Tish tucked her head into my neck as she trembled against me. I was stunned, wrung dry from the force of my climax. We stayed like that for long moments.

I savored the feel of her against me, soft curves, damp skin. I could feel her breath begin to slow along with mine and the tremors in her body begin to dissipate.

I sifted my fingers through her hair before my hand slid down her back in a slow pass. I felt as if someone had kicked my feet out from under me. I was off-balance emotionally. Everything that happened with Tish seemed to take me off guard. It was unexpected, startling, and raw.

When I felt her lift her head, I dragged my eyes open. We stared at each other. Even now, even after the force of the encounter had reached its climax, it felt as if something was still burgeoning between us. It was beyond sexual. It was beyond desire. I didn't know what to make of it, and I sensed she didn't either. This thing between us had its own life with the connection shimmering in the air between us.

She blinked before leaning forward and pressing a kiss in the divot at the base of my throat. The tiny touch felt like a brand on my skin.

I wasn't sure how, but I gathered up some composure. We managed to disentangle ourselves. Tish slipped into the bedroom to change into more comfortable clothes, while I stopped by the bathroom to dispose of my condom.

When she came back out, she stopped feet away, her gaze a little uncertain. She rested one foot on top of the other. I glanced down to see her toenails were painted purple. She followed my gaze.

"Teddy was napping the other day, so I painted my toenails." After a pause, she asked, "Do you want to stay?"

"You already asked and I did. Have you changed your mind?"

She shook her head quickly.

It was early-ish, but she looked tired. I reached for her hand. "Let's go to bed."

Once we were in her bedroom, she gestured toward the television on the dresser. "I didn't used to have a TV in my bedroom, but before Teddy started sleeping more, I needed something to keep me company. I'm lucky if I make it for six hours. It's nice to have the TV if he's restless."

"Lots of people have TVs in their bedroom," I pointed out before giving her a quick kiss.

A little while later, we had on a home improvement show. She said she liked the background noise. I didn't care what we watched. I just wanted to be with Tish.

She fell asleep within a half hour. When I woke up to a sound from the baby monitor, I glanced toward Tish. Her eyes opened instantly. She scrambled up just as I asked, "Do you want me to check on him?"

She swung her legs off the bed. "I'll check, but thank you."

A moment later, she returned to the bed holding a sleepy baby. She propped herself up on the pillows to nurse him. I sat up with her. "You don't have to do that," she said.

"I want to."

"You can sleep, Griffin."

I angled to the side to face her more fully. "Tish, I'm awake already."

Hours later, I came awake again. Tish didn't stir when there was a murmur of sound on the baby monitor. Slipping out of bed quietly, I went to check on Teddy. He bicycled his chubby little legs in the air when he saw me. I scooped him up, promptly discovering he needed a diaper change.

I was in the middle of that task when Tish appeared in the doorway. "Griffin."

Her hair was a wild mess and she was wearing a T-shirt and a pair of cotton shorts. I adjusted the last tape on the diaper and smiled over at her. "He needed a fresh diaper."

She studied me before laughing. Teddy rolled his head to the side and let out a squeal of joy when he saw his mom.

I handed him to her as she approached me. "I can't believe I didn't hear him on the baby monitor," she said.

"He didn't make much noise," I assured her. "I had to go to the bathroom anyway."

"Have you?"

I chuckled as I shook my head. "Now that you're up, I'll take this opportunity." I scooted past her.

A short while later, we were in the kitchen, and

Tish was holding the baby and trying to get the coffee made. "I got it." I nudged her to the side.

"You can't get everything!" she protested.

"I'm not. You've showered, you've dressed Teddy, you've gotten the bag ready for the day, and you fed him. All I've done is change his diaper and take my own shower. If we're going to keep track, which, by the way, I think is completely ridiculous, you're ahead. Let me make coffee."

I nudged her with my hip again and she sat down at the kitchen table. A few minutes later, I handed her a fresh cup of coffee before sitting down across from her. "Is there anything you want for breakfast?"

"Breakfast isn't something I have a lot of time for," she said slowly.

"I noticed you have some fresh eggs in the fridge."

She smiled. "Allie has chickens. They lay a lot of eggs."

"How do you like your eggs?"

"Griffin," she warned.

"Tish, I'm starving. I personally like scrambled eggs. Do you mind if I make some?"

She bit her lip to keep from laughing before shaking her head slowly. "Of course not. And, I love scrambled eggs."

After we finished eating, I cleaned up and filled the dishwasher. Without thinking, I started it. "Are you even for real?" she teased.

"Last time I checked," I quipped.

"Seriously. You change diapers, you make eggs, you clean up, what the hell?" she mused.

"I grew up with a lot of siblings and we all had chores. How are we doing on time?"

Chapter Twenty-Four

TISH

"Bye, sweetie. Mwah, mwah!" I gave Teddy exaggerated kisses before handing him over to the friendly woman at the daycare.

Teddy was easily distracted when she lifted him into the air and spun him in a circle. The daycare drop-off was going well so far. Although I experienced a few pangs of guilt, I was relieved he seemed to be adjusting well.

When I got into the office, Archer Cannon, Griffin's cousin, was talking with one of the contractors on the building project for the new distribution center.

"Hey, Tish," Archer called over.

When the contractor waved, Archer fell into step beside me as I walked toward my office. "How are things?" I asked.

"Good, I think. Everything situated with the guy who got injured on-site yesterday?"

"I already called over and checked in with him this morning," I replied.

"I am *so* grateful you're here," Archer said, his tone heartfelt.

I smiled at him as I walked into my office. "Yeah?"

"Seriously. All the HR stuff stresses me right out," Archer said flatly.

I dropped my purse on top of my desk and slipped out of my jacket. "Well, it's my wheelhouse, so happy to take care of it."

Archer's gaze arced around my office. "You know, you could make the space yours."

I looked around at the impersonal space. "I haven't had time. I needed to hit the ground running since I've been on maternity leave."

Archer narrowed his eyes at me. "There's a reason it's called "leave". I happened to know you were working for part of the time anyway. A baby is more work than work."

I burst out laughing as I rested my hips against my desk. "I'm actually relieved to be back at work-work. Don't get me wrong, I love Teddy more than I could've imagined loving any other human, but it's really nice to have adults to speak to on the regular."

Archer chuckled. "Phoebe said the same thing. I know some people want to be at home all the time with their kids. I like it in doses myself. Anyway, I wanted to get you up to speed on our planning for the year. We've got the project for the distribution expansion and the brewery and the restaurant. David is kind of our point person for the restaurant. He's usually in Fireweed Harbor, but he ran that restaurant for years as the chef. We could use all the help we can get."

"I've already been in touch with David. I know him from my time in Fireweed Harbor. Isn't the restaurant doing events already?"

Archer nodded. "Just events though. We've had so much interest, that we're pushing to get it up to full schedule. It's been so busy, and I just..." He lifted his hands in the air and let them fall.

"How about I just take that over? I'll coordinate with David, and you and Chase can focus on the distribution center, the brewery, and the renewable energy projects. I'm happy to help with anything."

"Honestly, if you can be on point with David, manage this entire office, and coordinate with HR on anything, we'll be fine."

"On top of all of that."

"If you want more furniture for your office, I can take you down to the storage space."

I glanced around in my bare-bones office, which at this moment consisted of a single desk and a small table in the corner. "I might take you up on that. By the way, who's going to handle the actual brewing here once it's up and running?"

My curiosity had nothing to do with Griffin, nothing at all.

"Hopefully Griffin."

"Oh," I said, striving to keep my tone as casual as possible.

"I can't imagine he'll be a firefighter that much longer," Archer added.

"Oh?"

"It's hard work. Phoebe did it for years. I had to manage my anxiety over it when we first got together. I'm relieved she only fills in for the town crew now."

I thought about Griffin being out in the wilderness fighting a fire. My heart pinched uncomfortably with a worry I hadn't even allowed myself to contemplate. It wasn't like we were a couple. I didn't need to worry like this.

"There you are!"

We glanced over together to see Phoebe standing

in the doorway. Her toddler squealed in excitement at the sight of Archer.

Archer beamed, immediately lifting the little boy from Phoebe's arms and spinning him in the air. Seconds later, he returned to Phoebe and gave her a lingering kiss. Her cheeks were pink when he straightened. "Nice to see you," she said.

When she looked my way, I waved. "Hey there."

"I wanted to see how work is going for you," she said.

"It's going."

Archer cut in. "I am so glad she's here. She's as amazing as Rhys said she would be. We had some time with her before, but we finally have her full-time."

"Of course, she is," Phoebe said confidently.

"I don't mind handling the messes and the boring admin," I offered with a shrug. "I appreciate that Rhys speaks so highly of me. I only hope I can live up to expectations."

Phoebe narrowed her eyes. "You're already exceeding them and you've only been here full-time for a few days."

Archer glanced between us. "I need to run down to grab a phone call in my office. Should I take Archie with me?"

"Go for it," Phoebe said with a grin. "I'll fetch him on my way out and drop him off at daycare."

She waved him off before glancing back toward me. "How is it really? The whole daycare back to work? On the one hand, I couldn't wait. On the other, it was stressful."

"That's exactly how I feel. I'm so grateful you recommended the daycare. Teddy seems comfortable there. He was a little fussy the first day or two, but he's adjusted quickly."

"Good. I knew it would be okay. Do you want to grab some coffee, maybe midday today?" she asked.

I was about to shake my head when she tipped her head to the side. "You're allowed to have breaks. I know from Rhys that you worked way more than expected when you were his assistant. Plus, you're still doing two jobs."

"Rhys hired a new assistant," I pointed out.

"Yeah, and you're onboarding that person and making sure everything goes as smoothly as possible. That's a job. Take a half an hour for coffee with me," she pressed.

A laugh rustled in my throat. "I will."

"I'll come get you here."

She waved as she left my office. I opened my laptop to a wall of emails. About a half an hour before I was going to meet Phoebe, I went to take care of my pumping for the day. Pumping my breast milk was decidedly not fun for me. After I put the breast milk in my small office refrigerator, Phoebe and I headed out for coffee.

As she was driving, I asked, "How long did you breastfeed?"

"Are you having mom guilt?" she asked wryly.

"Yes!"

"I feel you. I managed to stick with breastfeeding for nine months and that was it."

"I hate pumping. I am beyond grateful that I have my own office and I can do it privately."

"Well, I haven't talked to anybody that enjoyed pumping," Phoebe said.

I laughed.

"If there's one thing I've learned about being a mother, you're going to have about five million reasons to feel guilty about all kinds of things and you're constantly going to second-guess yourself and wonder if you're doing it wrong. You're also probably going to assume everyone else is doing it better or whatever. With all of that, try to cut yourself some slack. If you hate breastfeeding, stop. The world is filled with perfectly healthy babies who didn't breastfeed. Don't feel guilty. If we need to do an intervention on the mom guilt, we will."

Tears sprung to my eyes. I hadn't realized how good it felt to have friends who had my back. "Thank you. I'm not planning to stop breastfeeding just yet, but I'm thinking about it. Meanwhile, I'm trying not to feel like shit for actually enjoying going to work." Impulsively, I reached over and squeezed her shoulder, wanting to give her a hug. "Thank you for being so nice to me. I feel like I got a ready-made support circle when I moved here."

Phoebe slowed to turn into the parking lot at Firehouse Café. "You don't need to thank me. You're a good friend. What comes around goes around."

When we walked into the café a few moments later, my eyes landed on Griffin. He was at the back of the line, talking to another firefighter I'd met in passing. As soon as Griffin's eyes snagged mine, my belly did a little shimmy, and sparks spun like pinwheels through me.

Chapter Twenty-Five

GRIFFIN

"Oh, hey there, Griffin and—" Phoebe paused, her voice slowing. "I can't remember your name."

Hudson, one of the newer firefighters, cracked a quick smile. "Hudson Fox."

"That's it! I'd know your name if I was still firefighting full-time," Phoebe replied. She gestured from us to Tish. "Griffin, you know Tish, but Hudson, this is Tish, a good friend of mine and sort of new to town. She is now running the show for the offices here at Fireweed Industries."

Hudson dipped his head. "Nice to meet you, Tish."

I wanted to kiss Tish, right this very second. Her cheeks were pink, and I could tell from the uncertainty in her eyes that she wasn't sure how to greet me. This was a conversation we hadn't had. Maybe she was okay with us being public, but I didn't know.

Her lips curled in a smile as she glanced toward Hudson. "Nice to meet you."

Her eyes bounced to mine and away again, the flush deepening on her cheeks. She fiddled with the strap on her purse. Phoebe was saying something to

Hudson, so I stepped closer to Tish. "How's your day going?" I kept my voice low.

She peered up quickly. "Good. Yours?"

"Pretty good." I found myself wanting to ask her all kinds of questions, anything to keep her talking. I was also legitimately curious about how the planning with the brewery was going. "What is the time frame for the new distribution place to be up and running?"

Tish cocked her head to the side. "I need to confirm with Archer, but I think it's in about a year. So far, the restaurant is only open for events and all the alcohol they serve is from the production center in Fireweed Harbor."

Phoebe jumped in, "We're all impatient for the brewery." She nudged me with her elbow. "You're going to be the brewer, pretty please."

I chuckled. "Eventually."

After we ordered our coffees, I wanted to linger, mostly because I wanted to spend more time with Tish. While I was pondering how to do that, Nate Fox, a pilot who handled a lot of flights for hotshot crews, came walking in with his wife Holly. I'd met both of them briefly the other day.

"Hey, man" Nate said, clapping Hudson on the shoulder before pulling him into a back-slapping hug.

As Nate stepped back, I glanced to Hudson. "You two know each other?"

Nate waggled his brows. "We're cousins."

Holly lifted her hands to tighten her ponytail, her long blonde hair swinging when she released it. She glanced toward Tish. "How are you? Glad to be back at work?"

Tish smiled. "I'm struggling with guilt, but it's nice to be at work."

Nate looked between them. "Holly struggled with the mom guilt."

Holly rolled her eyes. "I'm so grateful we've made it to pre-school. I love it."

Nate slid his arm around her waist and gave her a lingering kiss on the side of her neck. Holly's cheeks went pink. It felt as if we were all interrupting them, but the moment passed. When I looked over at Tish again, my heart felt literally pulled in her direction.

I didn't think of myself as a romantic guy. I sure as hell didn't believe in fate. I was probably more cynical than the average person, especially when it came to family and relationships. Although all freaking six of my siblings were happily married now, our childhood had been filled with shadows and darkness. I'd been barely a toddler when our father had died unexpectedly. He and our mom had both been only children and they'd wanted a big family. That left our single, grieving mom completely overwhelmed when he passed. Our father's parents stepped in to help because they lived in Fireweed Harbor, and our grandfather had set in motion a series of events that left a trail of pain behind.

He'd been verbally and emotionally abusive to all of us and knocked our oldest brothers around with Rhys and Jake being his primary targets. Jake had buried his feelings in alcohol during college, and drank himself to death one night. It was only years after his death that we found out from Archer that our grandfather had also raped Jake. Archer had panic attacks for years until he finally talked about what he'd witnessed.

It wasn't all bad though. I was tight with all of my siblings and we took care of each other. A nice surprise in our messy family was discovering our half-brother, Chase. Our father had a relationship with another woman before he'd even met our mom, and she'd never told him she had a baby.

When Chase's sister signed them up for an online genealogy place, she'd found us. Although I had moved to Willow Brook for the hotshot crew, I was glad Archer and Chase were here.

"Griffin?" Tish's voice was soft.

I glanced down, realizing my mind had wandered far afield. "Yeah?"

"Your coffee is ready." She gestured to the counter.

"Thanks, Janet!" I flashed her a grin before stuffing a hefty tip in the jar.

Phoebe slipped over to Tish's side, sliding her hand through Tish's elbow. "We should get back to the office."

She glanced over at me. "Good to see you, Griffin."

I wanted to kiss her goodbye, but I checked the urge.

Nate, Holly, and Hudson were still there after Tish and Phoebe departed. Holly pinned me with her sharp gaze. "What's going on with you and Tish?"

"Uh, what?" I sputtered.

Hudson chuckled and Nate cracked a wide smile. "It's a small town, and Holly stays on top of everything."

"Why do you ask?" I hedged.

Holly rolled her eyes. "Because you couldn't keep your eyes off her and it's obvious you totally have a thing for her." The twinkle in her eyes took the edge off her bluntness. "Tish is a good person and you need to be nice to her."

I held Holly's gaze for a long beat before concluding honesty was the best policy. Maybe I didn't know if Tish was comfortable having anyone know anything about us, but I didn't mind being open about my feelings.

"I like Tish. A lot."

Holly tipped her head to the side, her eyes narrowing before a slow smile unfurled across her face. "Excellent. That's how it should be. Now, you better not be an asshole. I don't know enough about you to know if you are."

Nate cut in, "Slow your roll, Holly. He hasn't done anything to demonstrate he's an asshole."

"Maybe not, but you never know," she grumbled.

"I'm not planning to be an asshole," I offered.

"Well, what are you planning to do?"

Chapter Twenty-Six

GRIFFIN

Well, what are you planning to do?

I shook my head to myself when I considered Holly's question. My plan appeared to be hoping I would be able to see Tish again that very night.

Me: *Can I stop by tonight?*

I had to wait a solid half hour before she replied. I didn't even want to admit to myself that I felt impatient with the wait.

"She's working," I told myself as I finished a workout on the treadmill in the small gym at the fire station.

Tish: *I'd love to see you.*

I was smiling down at my phone when Chase's voice reached me. "Who's that?"

I glanced up, still smiling. "Just a friend," I hedged. "What's up?"

"Was thinking you should come out to dinner with me and Hallie soon? You can come to our place."

"I'd love that." As soon as I said that, I hoped he wasn't planning on tonight.

"You still staying out at Archer and Phoebe's place?" he asked.

"For the time being. I'm scouting around for some property or a house to buy."

"I actually know of one. It's down the road from our place."

"How about we pick a night for me to come out for dinner and I'll take a look at the place on the way over?" I asked.

"Sounds like a plan. Let me check with Hallie about when. With a kid, we gotta work around that," Chase explained.

"Do you know if it's listed with a realty place? I can check to see when I can schedule a showing and let you know. Of course, I can come out for dinner anytime."

Chase waggled his brows. He pushed away from the doorframe. "I'll text you, and maybe you can fill me in on that." He gestured toward my phone.

I chuckled, relieved he left it at that. I knew this thing with Tish was fresh, really fresh, but I didn't want her to be my secret.

———

That evening, I turned down the road that led to Tish's place, mentally clocking that it was pretty close to where Chase and Hallie lived. I shouldn't be wondering if I was going to buy a place near Tish, but I was.

A few minutes later, as I was walking up the steps at her place, the door opened and Allie came walking out. I'd seen her at the station a few times since our first encounter here. She narrowed her gaze when she saw me, eyeing me skeptically.

"What are you doing here?" She actually closed the door behind her and crossed her arms.

"Stopping by to see Tish. Is that okay?"

"I guess so," she grumbled.

The door swung open behind her. "Griffin is here to see me. He changes diapers," Tish offered with a grin.

Allie's expression relaxed a little. "Okay, then."

"Have I passed the test?" I teased lightly.

"Maybe," Allie said with a shrug as she jogged down the stairs. Seconds later, she rounded the side of the house to cut through a path in the trees.

I looked over at Tish, and for a beat, my heart seized before kicking fast. She looked beautiful. She was still wearing her work clothes, a fitted blouse that flared around her hips, and a fitted skirt that came to her knees. Electricity sizzled like fire through my veins. Her hair was pulled back tightly. I wanted to bend her over on the closest surface I could find.

Just as I was thinking that, the sound of Teddy letting out an irritated wail broke my train of thought. Tish spun around, tossing over her shoulder, "Come on in!"

I closed the door behind me, kicking off my shoes and hanging my jacket up before I followed her into the living room. Teddy was in his playpen. Tish leaned down to pick him up, and he immediately stopped fussing.

"He's tired," she explained when she glanced over.

Teddy's brow was furrowed and his cheeks were a little red. "How's daycare going?"

I stopped beside them, and he looked up at me, studying me for a beat before he curled his head into her shoulder.

"They say he's doing well." Tish circled her palm

on his back, murmuring in a soothing tone. "I just fed him. I predict he'll be asleep any minute now."

I watched as his eyes blinked before falling closed. "I think he's on the way."

"Let me put him down," she whispered before turning and walking down the hallway.

I felt as if she had a string attached to me. I wanted to follow her, but I didn't. I waited with leashed impatience.

"I forgot to stop by the store," she announced as soon as she returned.

I studied her for a beat before stepping close and doing what I wanted. I slid an arm around her waist and dipped my head to brush a kiss over her lips. "You could've asked me."

Her breath came out in a puff. "I'm adjusting."

"To what?"

"Teddy being in daycare, figuring out my work. I feel like I'm constantly forgetting something. Although honestly, I've felt like that since I had him."

"I bet. Being solely responsible for a human who's dependent on you for everything might lead to a little bit of pressure and a small adjustment in life."

She bit her lip as she smiled up at me. "Just a small adjustment."

"Let me see what I can scrounge up for food. I can always make more mac and cheese," I offered. "If you'd like me to run to the store, I'll do that."

"I feel bad about asking you to go to the store. I have mac and cheese and yogurt and oatmeal and a bunch of breastmilk." She waggled her brows.

I chuckled. "How about we do mac and cheese? I can go by the grocery store tomorrow."

"Griffin, you can't do all the things," she protested.

I held her gaze. "Tish, you're busier than me right

now. Any day now I might get called out to a fire. We're headed into the winter so that probably won't be the case. I'm doing training and getting to know the crew and admin stuff." I paused and took a quick breath. "Fuck," I muttered to myself.

"What?"

"I keep forgetting to take care of some HR paperwork. I hate doing paperwork."

"I love paperwork!" Her tone was so earnest I couldn't help but sputter a laugh. "I can do that while you make dinner. Or, I'll make dinner while you do the paperwork."

"I'll trade those tasks any day," I said with relief whooshing through me.

"Where is the paperwork?"

"On my front seat. Maisie reminded me today."

"You go get it. I'll start boiling the water." She grinned up at me.

I jogged outside to get it. Paperwork made me anxious. It didn't matter how many years it had been since I'd learned how to deal with dyslexia, it still stressed me out.

A few minutes later, Tish was working on my paperwork while I got started on the mac and cheese. She beckoned me over to give her some information. I sat down while the pasta was cooking. She traced her finger along the line before she glanced over.

"You seem really stressed about this paperwork," she pointed out.

I wanted to play it off, but I decided honesty was my best option. "I have dyslexia. It was a huge stressor in school for years until they figured it out. I know it has nothing to do with intelligence, but I still hate paperwork."

Her gaze softened. "My friend in school had

dyslexia. School wasn't fun." She shrugged. "Everybody's brain is a little different. We all have our strengths. I can't even imagine doing what you do. I can't keep my day organized since I've had a baby, but toss me some paperwork and I'll make a spreadsheet for you all day. I'll organize everything. Any time you need help with your paperwork, I'll help."

The tension in my chest eased. "It feels so stupid to care, but when I ended up behind in school and nobody understood why for years, it's always in the back of my mind." I could literally feel the tightening where the tension started to bundle at the base of my neck.

She nodded. "I bet. Like I said, I'll help. Now, let's finish this."

I recited the demographics she needed while she quickly entered everything in tidy handwriting.

"Thank you," I said with feeling.

"You're welcome." She leaned over and pressed a kiss on my cheek, just as the water began to boil over.

A few minutes later, we were eating and she smiled over at me. "This is mostly my diet. Mac and cheese, ramen, and soup. I need to expand my horizons somehow."

"You're a single mom with a baby. That's a lot of work."

"I don't mind the work. Not at all, but it's a lot. I was afraid to shower at first, which seemed crazy, but —" She rolled her eyes.

"Doesn't seem crazy at all to me. I have a question." I was nervous to ask this, but I knew I needed to.

"Ask."

"Do you want us to keep things with us private?

The other day at the coffee shop, Holly noticed I totally have a thing for you and asked me about it."

Tish was about to take a bite and lowered her fork. "Of course Holly would ask." She smiled sheepishly. Her cheeks went pink. "What did you tell her?"

Chapter Twenty-Seven

TISH

I felt hot all over and my pulse raced a little faster as I waited for Griffin to answer.

"I didn't tell her anything had happened, but I admitted I totally had a thing for you. Because I do."

The heat banked in his gaze lit sparks inside of me. Mingled within the desire that rose like a storm inside of me whenever I was near Griffin was a subtle anxiety. Back before I knew I was pregnant, I'd wanted to keep the boundaries clear. With Griffin's oldest brother my boss, all of my worries and anxieties had felt justified.

Rhys was still my boss, but more at a distance. Griffin was too tempting now for my anxiety to override my desire. I was still busy trying to tell myself it was mostly desire. My heart knew better and whispered as much in the back of my thoughts.

"Are we keeping this secret?" Griffin asked. His eyes held mine and my belly flipped while my heart kicked along unsteadily.

"I suppose I should ask what *this* is?" he added.

I needed oxygen so I could think and sucked in a breath as I set my fork down. "I don't know," I finally answered. "My life is kind of complicated. I have a baby and—" I paused, shaking my head sharply. "I didn't expect you, Griffin."

"I didn't expect you either, Tish. That first time I met you, even though I asked for your number, I figured I'd probably never see you again. What were the odds?" he mused.

I let out a soft laugh. "Probably not great." For the first time in a long time, I let my heart do the talking. "I don't usually do casual relationships. And –"

Griffin reached over, catching my hand, where I was nervously tracing along the side of the table between us. "I don't know what this is, or what we're meant to be, but you're not just casual for me. I'd like a chance to see where this might go."

My heart didn't even know what to do with those words, much less the intent look in his eyes. All I could do was whisper, "Okay. I'd like that chance too."

He squeezed my hand before lifting it and turning it over to drop a kiss in the center of my palm. If I hadn't been seated, I would've melted to the floor. He released my hand and the moment passed. We started to eat again, but I was still spinning inside.

While I was trying to get my body to cool down, Griffin pushed his empty bowl away and took a swallow of water, tracing his finger in a circle around the base of his glass after he set it down. "So, we didn't clarify one thing."

I finished my last bite. "What's that?"

"Are we keeping this secret?"

My mind wanted to say we should, but my heart didn't want that. And for once, my heart won. I shook my head.

Griffin's smile was slow and sent heat spiraling through me. Restless and a little anxious, I stood to put the dishes in the dishwasher. Griffin quietly helped me clean up. I finished drying my hands on the dish towel and turned to face him.

"Thank you."

He closed the dishwasher. "For what?"

"Making dinner again." I twisted the towel in my hands and rested my hips against the counter. "And, uh, having an actual conversation about us."

I wasn't devastated or brokenhearted by Paul disappearing from my life. We'd been at the beginning of a relationship. And yet, what he did created fractures in trust for me.

Griffin was quiet before he nodded. "You can thank Holly for that."

"Holly?" I snorted.

He shrugged, smiling sheepishly. "She made me realize this town is small enough that we should probably have that conversation."

He stepped closer, reaching for the towel in my hands and setting it on the counter before caging me between his arms. He leveled his gaze with mine as he leaned forward. His scent curled around me, a little crisp and woodsy. I didn't think I'd ever noticed how a man smelled before. Griffin was intoxicating, injecting a burst of oxygen into the fire already burning inside of me.

"You look beautiful today," he murmured as he dipped his head and grazed his teeth along the side of my neck.

"I'm just wearing my work clothes..." I gasped when he nipped at my earlobe and trailed his thumb over my collarbone. Every touch felt like licks of fire on my skin.

"I love your work clothes," he murmured. "I'd like to get you out of them as fast as I can though."

I could barely breathe and gasped something unintelligible just before he claimed my mouth in another hot kiss. By the time he lifted his head, I was practically on fire and had unzipped his jeans with my hand molded over his thick length.

"I need —" I began just as Teddy's cry came through the baby monitor.

I groaned. "Hold that thought. I'll be right back."

I ran down the hallway, sprinting through my bedroom into Teddy's nursery. He looked up at me, blinking his sleepy eyes. "Hey there," I whispered. I smoothed my hand over his hair.

He bounced his heels. I lifted him up to press a kiss on his temple. I loved the way he felt when he was tired, so soft and warm. He molded himself to me and maybe a minute passed before he was sound asleep again.

I held my breath when I eased him back into the crib, relieved when he stayed asleep. When I turned around to walk out, Griffin was standing in the doorway. He didn't say a word, he simply smiled and stepped back.

It felt like changing lanes in my body. As soon as the door was almost closed behind me, Griffin caught one of my hands and reeled me close, smoothly sliding his other arm around my waist and over the curve of my bottom. When I felt the swell of his cock against my belly, my sex clenched.

"Sorry about the interruption," I said breathlessly.

"Sweetness," he murmured along the side of my neck as he teased me with lazy kisses that sent shivers all up and down my body. "You don't need to apologize." He lifted his head, his gaze serious. "Although if you're not in the mood..."

I grabbed him by the back of the neck and pulled him down. "Don't make me wait."

I felt his chuckle against my skin. We yanked at each other's clothes, leaving them in a messy trail behind us as we stumbled to my bed.

Griffin set the baby monitor on the nightstand after I checked to make sure the door into Teddy's room was closed. I stopped at the foot of the bed, suddenly uncertain. I still felt almost out of place with my body. Having a baby had changed me so much. I had more jiggle than I'd ever had, and I was self-conscious about my stretch marks.

When Griffin sat down on the bed and turned me to face him, lightly cupping a breast and teasing his thumb over my achy nipple, I forgot my self-consciousness.

"You are so sexy to me, Tish," he murmured just before he sucked a nipple into his mouth.

I cried out sharply, my fingers spearing into his hair. For a split second, I thought I might orgasm right there. I felt so needy, so on edge. I gasped again when he teased my other nipple. He leaned back, bringing his fingers between my thighs and sliding them through the slick wetness there.

"Oh, sweetness. I've been wanting you since last night."

He sank a finger inside of me and my pussy clenched around it. "You have?" I gasped on the heels of a broken breath.

Another finger joined the first as he stretched me a little. "I sure have." I was trembling and panting, plea-sure sizzling in sharp streaks like little jolts of light-ning radiating through me.

"Griffin..."

"Tell me what you want."

"I need to come…" I gasped.

He kept his fingers inside of me as he leaned forward and brought his mouth to my sex. With this man fucking me with his fingers and teasing my swollen clit with his tongue, I stood before him desperate and nearly about to collapse. The pleasure was a storm whipping through me. I cried out when he pumped his fingers deeply, distantly hearing myself beg, "Griffin, please!"

With a subtle suction, pleasure broke in the eye of a storm. I barely remembered him drawing away, shimmying back as he brought me over him on the bed. I was kneeling astride him, staring at him as my climax still reverberated inside me. His cock was nestled in my folds. He rocked up, creating friction over my clit, giving me a little aftershock of pleasure.

"Give me a sec, I need to put this on," he said.

I couldn't even fathom that Griffin had the presence of mind to have a condom nearby. "Where did that come from?" I managed.

"My pocket."

I slid back, just enough for him to roll the condom on.

"I want you to come once more." He positioned his cock at my entrance, and I sank down over him, letting out a whimper at the indescribable pleasure of him filling me.

"Look at me, sweetness," he said.

I stared at him through heavy-lidded eyes.

"Just one more," he whispered before catching my lips in a kiss.

I could taste the subtle tang of my own essence on his tongue as he kissed me. He began to rock into me. My next orgasm built slowly, the echoes of it reverberating to my bones.

"Now," he ordered.

Chapter Twenty-Eight

GRIFFIN

Tish let out a whimper into our kiss, and I reached between us as I felt her tighten and begin to tremble. She rippled around me and I finally let go of my restraint, my own climax slamming through me so hard and fast.

I held her close, savoring the feel of her heartbeat thumping against my chest along with mine. Eventually, we disentangled ourselves.

Tish went to check on Teddy while I slipped into the bathroom and disposed of the condom. A little while later, when she was curled against my side, sound asleep, and I could feel the soft gust of her breath over my skin, I contemplated just how good this felt.

There was a piece to it that I didn't ever expect. I'd never expected this kind of closeness with anyone. My childhood had been disrupted with loss and abuse. Although I knew such a connection was possible, my heart was well-guarded. Or, so I'd thought. Tish slipped through my defenses like smoke sliding through invisible cracks.

I fell asleep and woke to the sound of a baby's cry.

Tish scrambled up, awake instantly. I had already started to sit up. "I can get him if you need me to."

She glanced over as she was swinging her feet off the bed. I could sense the hesitation before she said, "I could use a trip to the bathroom first. That would be great."

When I lifted Teddy out of the crib, I could tell instantly he needed a diaper change. I got started on that and felt Tish standing in the doorway a moment later.

"Almost done," I said. I powdered him and put a fresh diaper on.

"You didn't have to do that," she said, her voice still rough from sleep.

Lifting Teddy up, he curled against my shoulder before I passed him to her. "He needed a diaper change. No need to make him wait."

She studied me for a beat before leaning up and pressing a soft kiss on my collarbone. "Thank you."

A few minutes later, we were both propped up on the pillows in bed and Teddy was nursing. Tish rolled her head to the side. "You can go to sleep, you know."

"Teamwork makes the dream work," I teased. "I'll wait up with you."

Chapter Twenty-Nine

TISH

I must've fallen asleep while Teddy was nursing. I came awake when I felt him being lifted away. I dragged my eyes open, about to insist on getting up.

Griffin brushed a kiss on my cheek. "I got him. Go back to sleep," he whispered.

That was the last thing I remembered.

The next morning, he changed Teddy's diaper again. I was still settling into my new routine of a morning rush.

It was remarkable the difference to have someone else there to scoop Teddy up and put him in his playpen when he started fussing. Someone to help tidy up in the kitchen. Someone to wash the dishes when I didn't ask. It was shocking really.

Once again, I found myself thanking Griffin when we walked outside. His eyes flashed with his smile before he bent low to give me a kiss. As he was lifting his head, we heard the sound of tires on gravel. We glanced over together to see Graham and Madison pulling in.

Madison's smile was wide as she hopped out of the truck. "Good morning!" she said a little too cheerfully.

I could feel my cheeks burning up. Griffin seemed far less ruffled by this. "Morning," he replied with a nod.

Graham grinned between us. "We were driving by, and Madison wanted to stop."

As usual, Madison's glossy dark hair looked perfect and casually styled, and her gorgeous green eyes were bright. She managed to effortlessly look beautiful. It had taken me a bit, but I'd gotten over being intimidated by her beauty. She was a wonderful friend and had made my life so much easier since it had been turned upside down.

She shrugged. "I'm just being nosy. I saw the truck here and Graham said it was Griffin's, so..." She waggled her brows.

I tried to keep from laughing, but it came out as a putter. "I actually have to get to work. You can be nosy all you want, but can I fill you in later."

Madison chuckled before glancing toward my car to see Teddy in his car seat. I hadn't closed the door yet. She hurried over to give him a smacking kiss on his cheek while he kicked his feet in joy.

Madison closed the car door for me. "How's work going?" she asked as I was slipping my keys out of my pocket.

"So far, so good."

"I'll be in touch with you soon. I handle all the accounts for the construction projects here. I'm so glad you can be my point person," she said. Madison was an actuary and accountant.

"That's what Archer told me. We'll make a time to connect."

She nodded. "You're coming to card night, right? Allie will babysit."

"Of course. When is that again?" I asked.

"Tonight. It's Friday in case you lost track." She winked.

After they drove off, Griffin paused beside me. "Are you okay about that?"

"You mean them knowing we have a thing. It's fine." I bit my lip as I looked up at him. "Are you okay with it?"

"I like you, Tish," he murmured. "Kind of a lot."

He kissed me, leaving me needy before I drove away.

Blessedly, my day was busy, busy, busy.

Even though I was still adjusting to not being with a baby all day and missing Teddy and wondering how he was doing, I was enjoying getting back in the swing of things. Rhys's new executive assistant seemed to be handling everything very well. He pinged me with questions here and there, but otherwise, I was able to focus on my new position.

Later in the afternoon, Griffin texted to see how I was doing and asked if he could see me that night. I reminded him about card night with my friends and told him he could come by after that.

Griffin: *What time?*

My belly flipped.

Me: *Probably around nine.*

Griffin: *I'll be there.*

I was biting my lip as I smiled at his return text. I almost had a syncope episode. I was feeling a little lightheaded when I realized I hadn't eaten lunch yet and got up too quickly from my desk. Thankfully, no one was around. I sat back down and fished out my emergency candy to give me a little hit of sugar. That and a hard-boiled egg snack were enough to tide me over.

Chapter Thirty

TISH

Allie scooped Teddy out of my arms, giving him a loud kiss before lifting him in the air while he giggled. "He's all mine now, you relax," she said.

My heart clenched a little in my chest. When I'd first had Teddy, I'd been nearly desperate for any kind of break at first because it was a twenty-four-hour job. Babies didn't operate on a rational schedule. Days of endless diaper changes, nursing, and sleep doled out in hours here and there.

Now that Teddy had settled into somewhat of a decent sleeping schedule, usually only waking maybe once a night and I had returned to work, I missed him during the day. Yet, I also wanted and needed this time with my friends.

"We'll just be upstairs," Allie assured me. With a wave, she was gone.

Madison smiled over at me, her brows hitching up as soon as Allie was out of the room. "You okay?"

I took a quick breath. "Yes. But it's weird. I'm working now and I've only seen him for a few hours today."

Maisie had just walked into the room and her hand landed on my shoulder. She patted me lightly. "I know the feeling. Trust me, he's fine and you'll get used to it."

I smiled up at her. "Really?"

Her curls bounced with her nod. "Promise."

"Is Beck home with the kids tonight?" I asked.

"They're with his mom tonight. He's out with the guys at Wildlands. They kinda like to do that when we have our card night," Maisie explained.

Amelia sat down and slid a stack of paper plates into the center of the table. "They feel like they gotta have a guy thing because we have a girl thing."

"How long have you all been doing this anyway?" I asked as I took the plate that Lucy handed to me.

"Years now," Lucy replied.

Maisie nodded. "It was pretty casual at first, and more and more have joined in."

"Me!" Jasmine came walking with Susannah.

I felt blessed to have been welcomed so warmly into the group. Phoebe had smoothed my way, along with Hallie. Phoebe was here, but Hallie had texted me to let me know she was too tired tonight.

Amelia started shuffling cards. I passed on playing tonight. "I'm just gonna enjoy watching," I offered.

"You know how it goes," Susannah commented. "Maisie usually wins and sometimes Lucy."

Maisie waggled her brows. "I learned from my dad. He mostly ignored me, but he was really good at cards."

As the conversation carried on, Madison nudged me in the side with her elbow. "Yeah?" I glanced over.

"How are things with Griffin?" she asked.

Before I could reply, Phoebe's gaze bounced from me to Madison. "You and Griffin?"

. . .

My cheeks were burning up, so I didn't try to bluff my way through it. "We might be, um, seeing each other."

Phoebe's brows hitched before a slow smile unfurled across her face. "Griffin is a *great* guy."

My heart was pounding fast, and my belly fluttered just thinking about Griffin. "I know." I took a quick breath. "I think he's a little crazy because I have a baby, but he doesn't seem to mind." Most of them knew the story about Teddy's father.

"Is he helping?" Maisie asked as she studied her cards.

"With what?" I asked.

"With the baby. That tells you a lot about a guy."

"Actually, he is, and I didn't expect him to. He even does dishes and makes the best mac and cheese I've ever had," I offered.

"Well, that pretty much tells you everything you need to know," Lucy said before focusing on her cards again.

"I haven't known Griffin that long, but he seems like a good guy," Maisie added.

"Archer's known him since they were kids. He's great," Phoebe offered. "How do *you* feel about him?"

I felt a little put on the spot, but I trusted my friends and figured I might as well be honest. "It's pretty fresh, but since I have Teddy, I can't really imagine trying to do the casual thing. I also work for his family's company. He's not working there yet, but —" I paused, my face getting even hotter.

Madison waved dismissively. "Griffin doesn't even work there."

"I know, but he will eventually take over the brewery here."

Phoebe shrugged. "When you were Rhys's assistant, that might've been really too close for comfort, but not now."

While my friends were curious, maybe even nosy, I knew they all cared. I took a bite of my pizza. Just as I finished chewing, Madison nudged me again. "Griffin will be good to you."

I slid my gaze to hers. "I hope so."

"I see the way he looks at you. The man is smitten," she said firmly.

"He's probably at Wildlands tonight with the guys, and Chase or Archer is giving him a lecture about being good to you," Lucy chimed in.

"Graham will lecture him on my behalf," Madison said with a grin.

Chapter Thirty-One

GRIFFIN

I slipped my key fob out of my pocket, twirling it on my finger as I walked out to the parking lot. Graham was ahead of me, holding the door. "Thanks, man," I said.

"Of course." He released the door and it swung shut with a thump.

With it being autumn, the days were getting shorter. Even then, the last rays of the sunset were shimmering on the lake behind Wildlands Lodge.

Graham stopped beside the back of my truck. He waited just long enough that I assumed he had something to say.

"What's up?" I asked.

His lips twisted to the side. "You better be good to Tish."

"Of course," I said quickly.

He leaned his head back with a sigh before leveling his gaze with mine again. "I care about Tish, and I know a bit about being a single parent." I knew he'd raised his daughter mostly on his own until she was a teenager and Madison came along, so I nodded. "Allie asked me to warn you to be good to her."

I felt my eyes widen. "So, she'll kick my ass if I screw this up?" A laugh sputtered out.

Graham cocked his head to the side with a slight smile. "She will."

I studied him for a beat. "Well, you don't need to worry."

His gaze sobered. "I didn't think so. Buckle up: love isn't for the faint of heart."

I didn't even know what to think of his choice of *that* four-letter word.

My heart spun and kicked, while my mind stumbled.

———

Later that night, Tish shifted a little closer, curling her hand into mine. I traced my thumb along the inside of her wrist.

She dipped her head to dust a kiss in the little dip just below my collarbone. We fell asleep, and I woke at some point to discover the TV was still on with some cooking show playing. Tish was sound asleep, her leg thrown over mine. I carefully shifted to reach for the remote and turn the TV off.

The next time I woke, I was spooning around her. I was deeply aroused, my hard length nestled against the curve of her bottom. Her T-shirt had ridden up, and my palm was splayed on her belly. I sucked in a slow breath, willing my arousal to ease.

It surprised me when I heard her voice, raspy from sleep. "Griffin."

I smoothed my hand down her belly. "Yeah?"

She turned over and boldly stroked a palm over my

length. Just the night before, we'd had the birth control conversation and she'd told me she had an IUD. I was deeply relieved not to worry about scrambling to find a condom right about now.

My entire system felt piercingly alive at her touch. I let out a strangled sound. She stroked again. "I need you," she whispered.

In a fiery second, I was so close to the edge that my breath hissed through my gritted teeth. "Sweetness, you don't have to—" I felt the hot shock of her lips against mine before she moved swiftly, rolling me back and shimmying up to straddle me.

"I know I don't have to do anything. What if I want to?" she teased.

"Well, in that case..." My words were broken with a ragged groan when she rolled her hips over me. Nothing but my cotton boxers and her panties separated us. "You can have me."

Then, she was kissing me, and seconds later I was rocking deeply into her. She trembled and came all over my cock in the sleepy darkness.

———

With my feelings for Tish sharp in my mind and heart, it didn't surprise me when Wyatt called. I wouldn't say we communicated by telepathy as twins, but it did seem that we often knew when the other had something important to share.

"Hey, what's up?" I asked, answering the call when I saw my twin brother's name flash on the screen.

"I understand you have some news," he said, his voice teasing.

"Maybe," I finally said after a beat.

I had told Wyatt about my feelings for Tish back

when she had been trying to push me away, but I hadn't mentioned her since I'd moved to Willow Brook. As my twin, Wyatt knew me well and he knew I *really* liked her. But he'd said he understood her concerns back in Fireweed Harbor. "Tish works directly for Rhys. It would be awkward here in town for her," he'd said.

"I was planning to call you," I explained.

He chuckled. "Figured."

He and I texted a few times a week, but we saved the big conversations for phone calls or when we actually saw each other.

"So what did you hear?" I asked.

"Chase happened to call me about something to do with the equipment for the brewery there. He mentioned he thought you and Tish were official."

My lips tugged into a smile. "It's official. Does Rhys know?"

"I thought I would save that for you," Wyatt teased.

"I'll call him."

"Tell me something, are you in love with her?"

I took a quick breath. I pondered his question for a few seconds, even though I actually knew the answer. It was a gut check for myself as much for him.

"Yeah. I am."

"Well, that's good. I thought when she moved away, that might be the end of it."

"I did too. Who knew?"

He chuckled. "All right. Get that call over with because you know word will reach Rhys soon enough."

"I'll call him right after this. You and Rosie doing okay?"

"Amazing."

My cynical brother still sounded downright besotted with his wife. "You be good to her."

"As if I'd be anything but," he returned.

I was good to my word, and as soon as I finished my call with Wyatt, I called Rhys and filled him in.

"I thought you had a crush on Tish," Rhys replied immediately.

"You did?"

His dry chuckle filtered through the line. "It was hard to miss the way you looked at her. Figured it could've gotten awkward if she was still working for me directly, but she moved."

He paused, long enough that I prompted, "Rhys?"

"Be good to her."

My throat felt tight. "I will."

———

The following morning, Tish smiled at me over a cup of coffee. "After months of just me and a baby in the morning, it's really nice to have a grown-up here. That's not the only reason I'm happy you're here," she added in a rush.

Just then, my phone vibrated with a distinct tone. Her brows hitched up. "What's that?"

"Work. That means we have a call out to a fire."

Standing quickly, I gave Teddy a hug and Tish a lingering kiss before I hurried out to my truck and headed into town.

Our crew was called out to an unexpected late-season fire in a hunting area started by someone leaving a smoker unattended. Once I knew I'd be headed out of the area, I texted Tish, filling her in on the basics.

My thumbs hovered over the screen as the plane

was readying for takeoff. I wanted to tell her I loved her, but I didn't.

My thoughts spun to Graham's observation about love. I thought maybe he understood more than I did about this.

Me: *I'll miss you.*

Chapter Thirty-Two

TISH

I re-read Griffin's text a few times over the following days. I missed him. A lot. I was startled at how quickly I had become accustomed to his presence in my life.

Allie and Madison invited me over for dinner one evening. When I arrived, Allie gestured to a row of nail polish bottles on the table. "We're doing nails tonight," she offered with a grin.

"Really?" I looked at my neglected nails and laughed softly as I sat down at the kitchen table. "I could definitely use something to make mine look better."

"Madison taught me how to do nails better," Allie explained. "She also helps me with my hair, but I don't dye it myself anymore."

Madison set a casserole pan in the middle of the table. "Let's eat first. Do you want something to drink?"

"Just water," I replied. I had nursed Teddy before I came over and he was down for the count in his car seat. I loved how handy car seats were. Maisie had suggested I keep a car seat in the house because they made easy portable nap spots, so I carried him in his seat often.

With Allie checking on Teddy, we ate and chatted. I was bursting to ask how Madison handled Graham being a hotshot firefighter, but I held back. Once we finished eating and settled in to take care of our nails, Madison's eyes lifted to mine. "You'll get used to it."

"Used to what?" I hedged.

"Being with someone who flies out to the middle of nowhere to fight fires. Allie's dealt with it for years because Graham's been a firefighter since she was little."

"Did he always fly out?" I couldn't help but ask.

Allie was carefully painting my nails for me. She glanced up as she shook her head. "When I was little, he worked on the town crew. When I started high school, he switched to the hotshot crew. My grandparents are here in town, so I used to stay with them when he went out for fires. That was before he met Madison." Her smile was warm when she looked up quickly at Madison.

I was curious about Allie's mom, but I didn't feel like it was my place to ask. As if she could read my thoughts, she added, "My bio mom's never been around much. I was an unplanned high school pregnancy. She bolted after I was born. She visits once in a while, but hardly ever." Allie shrugged, but her gaze was somber.

"I'm sorry," I said quickly.

Pain flickered in her gaze before she glanced toward Madison. "It's okay. My dad's awesome when he's not driving me crazy and I've got Madison." Her eyes softened. "She's pretty great."

Madison smiled warmly. "I try."

As I contemplated if I should say anything else,

Allie shifted the track of our conversation. "I hope Griffin is good to you."

Heat flared in my cheeks. "He is so far."

Madison looked from Allie to me, her lips curling in a bemused smile. "Allie demanded that Graham warn Griffin that he'd better treat you well. I don't know if Griffin mentioned that to you."

I let out a disbelieving laugh. "Seriously?"

Allie finished one hand in the rich, maroon color she'd selected before switching to the other hand. "Griffin seems nice, but you deserve somebody to treat you well and so does Teddy. Griffin can't just be—" She waved a hand in the air before her cheeks went pink. "I don't know, casual."

I smiled, feeling my heart tighten in my chest. "That's really sweet that you want to make sure he's good to me. I appreciate it."

Allie studied me for a moment. "Do you like Griffin a lot?"

My heartbeat picked up its pace. I finally nodded. "I think I do. He's definitely not someone I was expecting. Teddy sure likes him."

"Is he good with Teddy?" Allie prompted as she focused on my nails again.

"He really is. He has a few nieces and nephews, so he's had a little practice with babies. That's a bonus." I glanced toward Madison. "Do you ever hear from Graham when he's out at a fire?"

"Not usually. There's not a lot of reception out there. Once they get closer to towns, we hear from them," she explained.

"Has he ever gotten hurt?" I couldn't help but ask.

Madison shrugged. "Not seriously, but a few minor things. They carry a lot of gear and the work is hard.

It's definitely a possibility, so you have to live with that." Her tone was practical.

Anxiety spun in my chest.

———

I thought about her comment over the following days. I was a little startled at how much I missed Griffin. The intensity of our connection was powerful. I felt as if the invisible bonds between us were tightening swiftly, the distance almost strengthening it.

He had been gone for over four days when I got a call from an unfamiliar number. My stomach started churning when I saw I had a voicemail. My thumb hovered over the voicemail, itching to hit delete. Nausea welled up when I eventually listened to the message.

It's Paul. I heard through the grapevine that you moved away from Fireweed Harbor. My parents want to meet the baby if it's mine.

Sheer panic surged inside. Part of me wanted to immediately call back and tell him to fuck right off. I had enough sense not to do that and decided to ignore his message until I had a chance to talk to an attorney. I wished Griffin were here because he would know what to tell me.

With anxiety churning like a storm in my chest, I dropped Teddy off at daycare. I managed to keep myself from completely falling apart until I got into my office and closed the door. I sat down at my desk with my hands shaking. I didn't want Paul to be involved in Teddy's life. I didn't trust him at all. I thought about calling my parents. They'd come up to visit a couple of times since Teddy was born. And yet, I'd kept the details about Paul vague because it was embarrassing. Even though I knew I'd done nothing wrong, I was still ashamed.

As I scrambled inside, my brain finally landed on Quinn Blackthorne. She was the lead corporate attorney for Fireweed Industries. She would know what to do. With my hands still shaking, I pulled up her number and called her.

"Quinn Blackthorn," she answered, her tone crisp.

"Um, hi, Quinn. It's Tish Reeves."

She must've heard something in my voice. "Tish? Are you okay?"

I cleared my throat, scraping for what little composure I could dredge up. "I'm sure you know I had a baby and the father isn't involved at all. But, um, I got a message from him this morning. He says his parents would like to meet Teddy. I don't want him involved at all! What do I do?" My voice was rising to a squeaky pitch.

"Okay, we'll figure this out. I can put you in touch with Colin, my cousin at our law firm. He handles all the family law cases. But first, breathe."

I forced myself to draw in a slow breath. "I'm sure I sound like I'm freaking out, I'm sorry. I just didn't expect this call."

"It's okay. I'm sure it's stressful," she said in a soothing lawyer tone.

"Do you mind giving me Colin's number?"

"Already planning on it. I'll reach out to him so he knows who you are. He's a good guy and an excellent attorney," she assured me.

"Thank you, Quinn."

While Quinn and I weren't that close personally, she had always been nice to me around the office. She was married to Kenan, one of Griffin's older brothers.

"If you don't hear from Colin this morning, zap me

a text and I'll nag him. Unless he's tied up in meetings or court, I expect him to reach out to you immediately," she added.

Seconds after we ended the call, my phone vibrated with her forwarding his contact information. Just as I saved it to my contacts, his call came through.

"Hi Colin, it's Tish. I'm assuming Quinn reached out to you," I said.

Colin's voice was warm. "She said it was really important that I reach out as soon as I could."

I quickly summarized the situation, ending with, "Paul hasn't been in touch at all, and I just don't trust him. Not after what he did." Although I'd had to force myself through it, I'd explained how I ended up pregnant.

"Grandparents don't have legal rights, but they can petition the court for visitation," he explained. "In this case, I strongly recommend we file to make sure you have full legal and physical custody. Are you opposed to the grandparents having visitation?"

"No, as long as Paul doesn't have a say. I was honestly relieved he hadn't responded to my message before. I decided to have my baby because I wanted to anyway, but I still don't trust him after what happened."

"So he's never responded until now?"

"This is the first I've heard from him."

"You're on strong legal ground, but he could try to be involved. I just want to caution you about that."

"I don't want child support. I want nothing from him," I said vehemently.

"I completely understand."

"I don't even want to respond," I added.

Colin was quiet for a beat before replying, "You

don't have to, however it's my experience that a response can minimize tension."

"I guess I didn't really consider him ever reaching out," I finally said.

"My suggestion would be for you to respond to the message, to get a sense of what his parents would like. If you're not comfortable with that, I'm willing to reach out to them first, but it may not be necessary. Think about it."

After I ended the call with Colin, I let out a heavy sigh and leaned back in my desk chair. I deeply wished Teddy hadn't been conceived in the accidental way he had. I knew I'd been taking a risk when I decided to go forward with my pregnancy. Paul's actions were a huge violation of my trust. In some states, stealthing was considered a form of sexual assault, although that wasn't the case in Alaska, not yet.

I'd known someday there would be questions from Teddy about his father. I also knew I'd mentally shoved those away, telling myself I had plenty of time to figure out how to handle that. When Paul hadn't responded at all, until now, he had made it easy for me to ignore what could happen.

My fury at the situation churned in my chest. Intellectually, I understood his parents wanting to know their grandson. But I didn't trust Paul, not even a little. I didn't know how to navigate this.

Chapter Thirty-Three

TISH

There was a light knock on my door. "Come in!" I called out.

Phoebe peered around the door. The moment she met my eyes, her smile faded. She stepped into my office quickly and closed the door behind her. "What's going on?"

I opened my mouth to hedge, to find a way to be socially appropriate. Instead, I burst into tears.

Phoebe was at my desk in a flash, rounding it to lean down and hug me. "What happened?" She stepped back, lingering beside my desk, her worried gaze patient.

I took a sniffling breath. She reached for the box of tissues on the corner of my desk, handing me one quickly. I blew my nose before looking at her again. I tried to smile, but my lips wobbled.

She sat down in the chair across from me. "You're not prone to bursting into tears. Tell me what's going on. Can I help?"

I blew my nose again and wiped the tears off my cheeks. I had been vague about Teddy's father. I studied her for a moment, trying to gather my nerve. Although I knew in my gut what he'd done was a huge violation, it seemed small. I knew minimizing and dismissing the actions of men was par for the course. It often felt like the world wanted us to give shitty men a pass.

"You know how Teddy's father ghosted me?"

Phoebe nodded. "Yeah. Asshole."

"He's definitely an asshole. In a way, it's been a relief because I didn't have to deal with what to do if he didn't ghost me. You know how I got pregnant. When I confronted him, that was the last time we talked. I have crazy mixed feelings about it, I don't know what to do." I sighed and shook my head almost to myself.

When I glanced up at Phoebe, she looked calmly furious. "He's a fucking asshole, but we already knew that. Did he say where he was in his voicemail?"

I shook my head. "He's a commercial fisherman. Well, he was. I don't even know if he is still doing it, but he was in Fireweed Harbor for the fishing season when we met." I shrugged. "Anyway, all he said was his parents want to meet Teddy. I just got off the phone with Colin Blackthorne."

"Colin will handle it for you. He's a good attorney," she said firmly.

"I'm sure he is. I just don't know what to tell Paul's parents. I'm not against them having contact, but I don't want them to pressure me around Paul."

"Tell them what happened. Their response will tell you what kind of people they are," she said.

"That's a good point," I said slowly.

"Tell me if I'm being pushy, but I think you should just go ahead and call. I'm a run-straight-at-the-problem kind of person."

I smiled over at my friend. "You're also a trained hotshot firefighter."

Phoebe's eyes twinkled. "What do you think?"

Just as I was contemplating if I had the nerve to make that call right now, my phone vibrated with another call. As soon as I glanced down at the screen, the anxiety and nausea that I was barely keeping at bay started churning at high speed.

"Who is it?" Phoebe pressed.

"Paul," I said flatly.

After the call went to voicemail, I stared down at my phone as if it were a venomous snake about to strike. "You think I should just play the message?"

"Play it." Phoebe's calm tone helped me.

Nausea burned my throat as I tapped the screen and hit play. *Just to follow up, I don't want to be involved, but my parents do. I'll file for custody if I need to so they can have visits.*

Phoebe's eyes narrowed, flashing with her anger. "What a fucking loser. You've already talked to Colin. Let him handle this."

———

I got through my day, telling myself it would be fine, that somehow Colin would straighten this out for me. I'd updated Colin about the second message from Paul and provided his contact information.

Late that afternoon, he called me with an update. "He's worried about child support," Colin said.

My laugh was bitter. "I don't want any money from him, but I want everyone to know the truth."

"About how you got pregnant?" Colin prompted.

"Yes. His parents can have visits, but they'll have to hear why I don't want Paul involved."

"Understood."

I felt so stupid, so painfully stupid. This whole thing brought up so many feelings of shame and embarrassment.

That night, I missed Griffin. Badly. I missed him most of the time, but I was able to put it to the back of my thoughts when I was busy at work. But tonight, my heart ached with it. I wanted his strength, the way his presence comforted me.

I didn't know when he would get my text, but I sent it anyway.

Me: *I miss you.*

Chapter Thirty-Four

GRIFFIN

I re-read Tish's text with my heart kicking against my ribs.

I slung my jacket over my shoulders as I walked down the back hallway in the station. We'd landed back in Willow Brook this afternoon. I'd been planning to text and see if I could stop by to see her, but I decided to surprise her.

"In a hurry?" Chase asked as I walked out to the parking lot.

I paused beside my brother. "Headed to see Tish."

He studied me for a beat, his lips twitching at the corners. "Never seen you like this. You know there's a bet out there."

"On what?" I narrowed my eyes.

"When you might settle down. You're the only sibling who hasn't."

As recently as six months ago, I would've scoffed at this. Although my passing encounter with Tish when we first met had been powerful, it had seemed like a fluke, almost a mirage. While my draw to her at the time had been startling and unexpected, I certainly hadn't been thinking about marriage, or getting serious.

Hearing the entirely not-surprising fact that my siblings were betting on when I might get serious with someone, I simply shrugged. "When the time is right."

Chase chuckled just as Hudson came walking out of the back doorway, almost running into Chase. Chase stepped to the side. "Everybody's in a rush today."

"We've been out at a fire for two weeks. I'm looking forward to some food that isn't freeze-dried," Hudson said dryly. "You guys headed to Wildlands?"

Chase thumbed toward me. "Griffin's headed home to his new girlfriend, and I'm going straight home to my wife and kid."

"Smart move." Hudson winked as he walked on by.

I tugged my keys out of my pocket. "See you soon."

As I began to walk away, Chase called, "Dinner with me and Hallie soon?"

"Anytime. Except tonight," I added.

He grinned. "Wasn't planning on that tonight. I need Hallie all to myself."

The drive to Tish's place was maybe ten minutes. Impatience gnawed at me through every minute of every mile. When I turned down the driveway, I was relieved to see her car there.

Moments later, when Tish opened the door, I could instantly see the distress in her eyes. She was holding Teddy, and I immediately reached for him. "What's wrong?"

She opened her mouth to say something and burst into tears. I held Teddy with one arm. He curled into my shoulder as I reached around and pulled her close, kicking the door shut behind me.

Tish's storm of tears passed quickly. When she lifted her head, she took a shaky breath.

"Paul reached out. He says his parents want to know their grandson. I called Quinn and she put me in touch with Colin. I'm freaking out because I don't know how I'm going to pay for all this and..." She stepped back, letting her face fall into her hands as she took a shuddering breath before her hands fell away. "I don't mean to dump all this on you the second you showed up."

Teddy squealed and I glanced down at him. I lifted him high in the air, giving him a quick spin to distract him before lowering him back down. "You're not dumping anything on me. What's the status on dinner for him and you? Let's take care of one thing at a time."

"I've only been home a few minutes. I'm so frazzled that I can't even think. I know they do a late afternoon snack at daycare, so I should feed him and —" She let out a flustered sigh.

"I'll get him a bottle and let's just order some takeout. No fuss. You've had a long day."

Her lips curled in a sheepish smile. "I didn't even know you were coming back today."

I adjusted Teddy in my arms as I stepped close again. "I would've texted you, but I decided to just come straight here. I missed you," I whispered against her lips before giving her a lingering kiss.

She blinked back tears when we broke apart. "I missed you too. A lot."

"You don't need to cry about that," I teased lightly.

I could hear the shakiness in her breath and protectiveness rose swiftly inside. I didn't expect what I said next. "I love you."

Tish's eyes widened, shining with tears. "Oh!" Her

hand was resting on my chest and pressed harder before her fingers curled into the fabric of my T-shirt. "I love you too," she whispered.

We stared at each other. I could see my surprise reflected back in Tish's eyes.

"We didn't really plan this, did we?" I mused.

She shook her head. "Not even a little. I certainly didn't expect the random guy I met on the side of the highway to end up here with me."

The moment was broken when Teddy kicked his feet against my thigh. Tish moved to reach for him. "I've got him," I said. "You order pizza. You know I'll eat anything, so just pick whatever you want. I can feed him."

I could see the weariness in her eyes. "This is why you pump at work. Order the pizza and hop in the shower. You'll feel better."

Her weary smile made my heart thump harder. "Thank you," she whispered.

A short while later, Tish had put Teddy to bed, pizza had been delivered and eaten, and I was tidying up the kitchen. We even had a brief conversation about her stress about Teddy's father. The fact that he cavalierly called her like that infuriated me. He had no right, none at all. But I knew that wasn't how it looked from a legal perspective.

I was relieved Colin was already involved. I trusted him to handle it.

When Tish hung the dish towel up and turned to face me, I rested my hands on the counter beside her hips and dipped my head to kiss her. Our tongues tangled lazily. She reached between us, dragging her palm over my lengthening cock.

"We don't need to do this tonight," I whispered.

I knew she was tired and feeling emotional for reasons that had nothing to do with us.

"I know, but I want to. I missed you." She curled her hand around my neck, arching up to meet my lips for another kiss.

It was messy. Everything moved swiftly with an intensity of emotion whipping the flames burning between us higher and higher. Her gaze held mine as the air shimmered around us when I filled her with a deep thrust. I savored the way she clenched around me and cried out. My own release crashed through me and we trembled together. I held her close, whispering, "I missed you. I love you."

After we fell asleep and Teddy's cries woke me through the baby monitor, I carried him to her and waited up with her while she fed him.

After she fell asleep, I brought Teddy back to his crib. Once I slipped under the covers, I leaned over to check the baby monitor once more. As I settled into the pillows, a sense of comfort and rightness gusted through me. It felt as if everything was how it was meant to be.

Chapter Thirty-Five

TISH

"I'll have..." I paused, lightly tapping my fingertips on the edge of the counter as I scanned the chalkboard behind the counter at Firehouse Café. "A mocha."

"Do you want anything to eat?" Janet asked as she began prepping my coffee.

"I'll take a cranberry orange muffin."

Janet deftly adjusted the knobs on the espresso machine with one hand while reaching for a muffin with the other and putting it in the toaster. Just then, I heard Hallie's voice behind me.

"Hey, hey!" She stopped at my side, curling an arm around my shoulder and giving me a quick squeeze. "How are you?" She had a sly twinkle in her eyes.

"I'm pretty good. How are you?"

Despite the earthquake Paul's phone call had set loose inside of me, Griffin and I had a few good nights together and I felt more settled. I told myself denial was a perfectly acceptable coping skill when under stress. It also helped that Colin told me he would handle it and I trusted him. As much as I liked to manage things, in this case, I was simply handing over the entire problem to him and hoping for the best because I didn't know what else to do.

"I'm fine. How are things with Griffin?" she asked as her arm slid away from my shoulders and she waggled her brows.

I felt the heat rising to the surface of my cheeks. I couldn't even keep myself from smiling. I cleared my throat. "Good. Actually, really good."

Her smile widened. "I'm glad to hear that. Griffin is a great guy."

"I know," I said, thinking of how he got up with me during the night and dozed on the pillows beside me while I nursed Teddy.

Phoebe came in, followed by Maisie, Amelia, and Madison. We ended up deciding to get a table. I had a little cushion of time before I needed to be in the office. When we sat down, I experienced a sensation that was becoming familiar, a brief moment where I felt like I had forgotten something extremely important.

I gave my head a little shake, and Amelia noticed. "What is it?"

"Ever since I started going back to work and taking Teddy to daycare, this weird thing happens where I'll think I forgot something, but I didn't. He's basically been an extra limb for months. It's a little weird not having him with me all the time. I love him, but it's nice having a little break."

Amelia nodded vigorously. "I totally get it. I thought I was going to climb out of my skin after the first few months. I was so relieved that I had my mom and Cade's parents to help. Without them..." She let out a hearty sigh. "I don't know what I would do."

"My mom came up for two weeks at the beginning,

but she's still working so she can't be here full-time. I bet it's really nice having your parents close," I replied.

"It is, but we still do daycare. They all have things going on and they work. I am *not* cut out for the stay-at-home mom thing. I feel like I'm a much better mom when I'm working. Don't get me wrong, sometimes I am really freaking tired, but I can enjoy it more and not feel burnt out on it," she explained.

I smiled over at Amelia. "I love your take. That helps me with my guilt."

The conversation carried on. I didn't know why, but a sense of unease slid through me a few minutes later. I checked my watch, noting I needed to leave for work soon. I glanced around the table before looking toward the doorway to the café. My stomach plummeted and nausea rose in my throat.

"Are you okay?" Phoebe asked from my side.

I swallowed through the acid burning in my throat. "That's Paul," I whispered under my breath.

Chapter Thirty-Six

TISH

A few minutes later, I stood in the parking lot beside my vehicle. My arms were crossed tightly and my eyes pinned on Paul.

"I thought we should talk," he was saying.

"Paul, you ignored my texts. It's been over a year. You can't just show up like this and demand to be involved. You can talk to my attorney."

"Come on," he cajoled.

"No. You know how I got pregnant and I don't intend to hide it. I'm not opposed to your parents being involved." I paused and tried to breathe. "You're not calling the shots. You have my attorney's number."

Just then, Griffin's truck pulled up beside my car, a little gravel kicking up behind his tires. In seconds, he was by my side. "Leave Tish alone," he said, his tone low.

"Who the fuck are you?" Paul countered.

"That's none of your fucking business." I could feel Griffin's anger rippling under the surface.

"I can deal with this," I said under my breath.

He glanced to me quickly, fury burning in his gaze.

His anger wasn't directed toward me, but I felt like he was stepping in too fast and trying to take over.

Paul glanced between us, his eyes narrowing. "What? Are you two a couple?"

I didn't want to have this conversation with Paul. I was furious with him for showing up like this and didn't trust him, not even for a second. "That's none of your fucking business," I repeated Griffin's comment.

Paul studied me for a few beats. "I'll talk to your lawyer. I don't want anything to do with your baby, but my parents do, so this is for them."

As he drove away, I was shaking. Griffin curled an arm around my shoulders. "Colin will handle this. Phoebe called me, if you're wondering why I'm here," he added.

I took a slow breath. I couldn't make sense of my feelings. I was relieved Griffin was here, but it also felt as if all of this was spiraling out of control. Much as I loved Teddy with my whole heart, a baby was a shocking lesson in learning how much you couldn't control. One tiny human ran my life now and I was terrified Paul's interference might hurt us.

"I have to go to work," I said.

Griffin looked like he wanted to say more, but I just didn't have it in me to deal with anything else.

GRIFFIN

Tish: *Rain check for tonight? Bad headache.*

My eyes scanned her text again. I wanted to argue the point, to tell her I would make dinner for her and feed Teddy. I would make sure she could rest quietly. But I knew she needed time to herself. Though it literally made my heart ache, I had to back off.

Me: *Of course. If you need anything, text me and I'll be there.*

Hours later, I was trying to ignore my cranky mood. I was at Wildlands Restaurant & Bar with some of the guys from the station.

"What's up?" Beck asked from my side.

I glanced his way. "Hanging out with you guys," I said with a chuckle.

He cocked his head to the side. "You seem like, I don't know, like you're worried about something."

"Buckle up for some life advice," Graham offered dryly from across the table.

"Life advice?" I countered.

"Beck loves to offer life advice. And, honestly, he's pretty good at it."

I glanced back at Beck. "Tell me something: when Maisie has a headache, how do you handle it?"

"This early in your relationship, I'd say you need to work on your bedroom skills." He gave an exaggerated brow-waggle with that.

I almost choked on the swallow of beer I'd just taken. "That's not what I meant. I think Tish legitimately has a headache. She had a stressful day and she's got a baby at home. Do I push it and try to go over, or do I give her space?"

A motion caught my eye, and I glanced over to see Paul, fucking Paul, walking in.

"Whoa, what did that guy do to you?" Beck asked as he followed my gaze.

I ignored him, standing and threading my way through the tables. I stopped beside Paul. "You better fucking leave Tish alone," I warned.

Paul spun around. "What's it to you?"

"You can't just show up in her life like this."

"I can and I am. I'm my only hope for my parents to have a grandchild. They have one now, so you can fuck off," he retorted.

I wasn't prone to losing my temper, but the guy's proprietary attitude about Teddy and the way he just didn't give a fuck about Tish infuriated me.

I clenched my fists. "Why the fuck are you here now?"

Paul smirked. "If I file for custody of the baby, I stand to inherit plenty of money from my parents. I'm not above that." His tone bordered on cold.

I reached to grab his shirt, and he stumbled back. "Fuck off!"

Before I could make matters worse, I felt a hand on my shoulder and glanced back to see Beck. Graham was with him, and it was his hand on my shoulder.

"Griffin, he said, his tone low. "You don't want to be stupid."

When I looked back and saw Paul still smirking, I barely managed not to bury my fist in his face. Beck stepped in and forcibly walked Paul away. In the jumble of moments that followed, Graham was asking who Paul was when Madison arrived.

"That's Teddy's fucking sperm donor," I spat out. "Complete asshole. He wants nothing to do with Teddy, but he's filing for custody because his parents want to have a relationship with their grandson. He even said it's for the money."

Madison glanced over to where Paul was walking out the back of the restaurant, her eyes angry enough to spit fire. I began to follow him again, only to have Graham grab me by the collar and yank me backward.

"Dude, I'm all about punching that guy, but don't be stupid. In this case, take the high road. Use all your anger to support Tish."

I breathed in slowly. Graham marched me back over to the group and I glanced down at Madison. I couldn't help but wonder how much Madison knew. Paul was a piece of work. Madison was saying something to Graham, and Beck stopped beside me just as Cade approached.

"Don't be as stupid as me," Cade said dryly.

"What do you mean?" I asked.

"I was a dumbass and got in a scuffle with Amelia's ex."

Beck nodded and rolled his eyes. "People still say the only reason Cade didn't get charged is because his dad is the police chief. But Amelia's ex is the one who started the whole thing."

Cade grimaced. My adrenaline slowly dissipated. I

felt like an idiot because I let Paul get the best of me. Losing my temper just made me look like an ass.

Later that night, I glanced around the efficiency apartment above Archer and Phoebe's garage. Archer and Phoebe had made it clear I could stay here as long as I wanted, but that's not what I wanted. It was only one night without her, and I missed Tish so fucking badly.

Her place felt like home. Or, maybe it was Tish and Teddy that made it feel like home.

Me: *I hope you're feeling better. Missing you tonight.*

I felt foolish about almost losing my temper with Paul. He'd been goading me, and I knew better.

A sigh gusted out as I rested my elbows on my knees and tunneled my hands through my hair. My phone vibrated and I moved swiftly, spinning it around on the coffee table in front of me.

Tish: *I miss you too.*

My lips curled in a small smile. It wasn't much, but it was something. I saw the gray dots appear in the screen, indicating she was still texting.

Tish: *Madison told me what happened at Wildlands. I know you're just trying to help, but I have to deal with this myself. You might not understand why, but I think until I have this sorted out, we should take a break. I need some time.*

Me: *What do you mean a break?*

Chapter Thirty-Eight

TISH

"What do you mean?"

"Well, this is an unusual situation," Colin explained. "You're willing to permanently forgo child support. Paul's insisting that he wants to pay child support. He doesn't want any visitation with Teddy, except for his parents. But he doesn't want you to disclose what happened to them."

"Colin, Paul's only doing this because he wants financial support from his parents. He believes he'll get it this way. I think he's trying to make it seem like he's a caring father when he's not." I swallowed through the tightness in my throat. It felt like I'd been on the verge of tears for days at this point. "I just want to tell them the truth. They can visit Teddy, but I don't want Paul involved and I'm telling them the truth. Can you arrange a meeting?"

"Tish—" Colin began.

I cut in. "I know it's probably crazy but it's what I want to do."

"Okay, I will reach out to their attorney. Where would you like to meet?"

"Somewhere neutral. I know your office is in Fireweed Harbor, but I'll fly there if I have to."

"Actually, one of our paralegals is moving to Willow Brook. With Fireweed Industries expanding its presence there, we're getting a lot more business from that area. Stella will primarily work from there. She flies into Willow Brook tomorrow. If you don't mind meeting with her, we can arrange it so you don't need to travel."

Tears burned in my eyes again. I was a ball of emotion these days. This small kindness was almost too much.

"Tish?"

I cleared my throat. "I'm here. That would be great. If you give me Stella's number, I'll text her and she can reach out when she's here. Does she have a place to stay?"

"To start, she'll be staying in a small apartment we found for her with a little help from Archer and Chase."

"Oh, great. Should I pick her up at the airport?"

"No need. She's got a rental car. How about you meet her at Firehouse Café? Stella will make all the arrangements with the grandparents. You don't need to talk to them. I would prefer if you write down everything you plan to tell them, so you and I can discuss it."

"I understand you want to protect me, but I feel fine about this," I insisted. Telling the whole story was about the only thing I felt at peace with, which was a relief.

Colin was quiet for a beat and I could hear a light tapping sound as if he was drumming his fingertips on his desk. "For what it's worth, their attorney has been nothing but above board and has assured me they're acting in good faith. I'm familiar with the attorney they hired in Juneau and he's a good guy. He doesn't play games. He won't do something sketchy on their behalf. I'm not familiar with Paul's attorney, although I can tell he is confused by Paul's request. I'll text you Stella's number."

As promised, Stella's number came through a moment later. I immediately texted her. After I closed out that text window, I stared at the last one I had received from Griffin.

Griffin: *I miss you. I understand you want this time, but I want to be able to be there for you. I know this can't be easy.*

He'd sent this late last night. I must've read it about a hundred times. I missed him, so much my heart felt raw from it.

Even now, I didn't completely understand why I had asked for some space. I felt overwhelmed and deeply distressed about Paul's reappearance in my life. Paul made me question my judgment so much. I didn't regret, not even for a second, having Teddy, but I hated the shame I felt about how easily Paul had tricked me into thinking he was a decent guy. I couldn't help but wonder if I still would've been involved with him if he had never pulled that little stunt, and if I had never confronted him about it.

I knew I owed Griffin a reply.

Me: *I miss you too. I'm sorting out the situation. I promise.*

I was so embarrassed about Paul, and I didn't feel like I deserved Griffin. I shook my head quickly, trying to physically knock my thoughts off track. I didn't have time to get caught in the repetitive loop of recriminations and embarrassment.

My phone rang and Stella's name flashed on the screen.

I answered so quickly I almost broke my finger. "Hello!"

"Hi, Tish?" Stella prompted.

"Yes, it's me!" I forced myself to breathe. "I mean, this is Tish," I said a little more calmly.

"Hi, I was calling to explain I'll be in town this afternoon. I've already communicated with the grandparents' attorney, and they are in Willow Brook. If you want to do this meet and greet this afternoon, let's go for it."

"Whoa," was all I could manage.

"Is that too soon?" Stella asked.

My cheeks were raw from me chewing on the insides. "I kind of want to just get it over with. Where should I meet you?"

"How about we meet at the law office?"

I forcibly released the pen I was gripping tightly and set it down. I flattened my palm on the desk as I tried to slow my breathing.

"The office is neutral. I'll be there with you," Stella assured me.

"Paul won't be there?"

"We've made it very clear with the grandparents' attorney that if they violate that condition, there will be no meeting. This is a time for you to tell them what happened. If everything goes well and you're comfortable, we can set up a time for them to meet Teddy."

I released the air trapped in my lungs in a gust. "Okay."

"I'll see you in a few hours," Stella replied.

"Great," I replied, even though it wasn't great at all. Just as she was about to end the call, I prompted, "Stella?"

"Yes?"

"Thank you."

"Of course. This isn't an easy situation. You're giving them a lot of grace." Her voice softened with her response.

"I'm trying. Thank you, and I'll see you this afternoon."

Seconds after I finished the call, my phone vibrated with an incoming text.

Griffin: *I'm here whenever you're ready.*

My heart cartwheeled in my chest and tears pricked my eyes. I couldn't let myself get too emotional today. I had to keep it together, but it helped more than he could ever know that he was in my corner.

A few hours later, I waited in the parking lot at the small office building beside Firehouse Café. My palms were clammy and my heart was clanging in an anxious beat. I just wanted this to be over. A car pulled up beside me. The woman who must be Stella smiled and waved as she climbed out quickly, slinging a backpack over her shoulder.

I hopped out. "Stella?"

"That's me." She thrust a hand out.

"Tish," I said, releasing her hand after a strong shake.

Stella was adorable. She had big brown eyes framed with thick lashes. Her blond hair was a riot of curls barely contained in a ponytail. She was short with curves. She wore an unzipped down jacket over a blouse paired with leggings tucked into practical boots.

"We've got twenty minutes before they're supposed to arrive, so let's get in there," she said.

I followed her into the office. She locked the door

behind us, glancing over her shoulder to add, "We don't want them to just walk in."

She led me into what appeared to be a conference room with an oval-shaped table and chairs.

"Do you just handle mostly family cases?" I asked as she hustled around, tucking her backpack away and getting out some paperwork.

Stella shook her head. "Oh, no. I'm a paralegal for all the things. Blackthorne Law is busy. Colin handles the family law cases, and Quinn handles all the corporate stuff for Fireweed Industries. Her parents manage a few cases, but not many these days. We're very busy. I'm not the only paralegal, but I'm the only one who was willing to move to Willow Brook. I'm just about done with law school. This is a great gig for me. They've already promised me I can have a position with them as a lawyer once I'm done." Her dimples peeked out with her smile.

"That's awesome! I know Quinn pretty well because I used to be Rhys Cannon's executive assistant for Fireweed Industries. Now, I handle the office management here at this location."

"Quinn is amazing. She's my heroine and I want to be just like her," Stella enthused.

I chuckled. "You do?"

"She's so smart and on top of everything and I have so much respect for her. Of course, I respect everybody at Blackthorne Law, but except for her, they're all men, so..." She shrugged.

Within minutes, Stella had made coffee and we were seated at the table. She placed a notebook, two pens, and several folders in a row in front of her.

"What are those for?" I asked.

"Colin prepared several options for legal agreements. We'll see how you feel after the meeting.

There's no pressure to make a decision today. If you have any hesitation at any point, all you have to do is look at me and—" Pausing, she gestured to a pair of pens, one blue and one black. "Blue means you want to wait, black means you're ready to go. Just pick up the one that works for you. I'll handle the legal talk, so don't even worry that you have to explain anything."

"Oh, that makes it easier." My chest was still tight, but I was feeling better.

"I know you reviewed everything with Colin, but is there anything else to cover before they get here?" she asked.

"Nope."

Stella's presence had this amazing effect on me. She was cheerful, almost bubbly, but also completely professional. She oozed competence and I felt like I was in good hands with her. I had zero doubt she would have my back if I needed something.

"I'm ready for them to get here so we can get this over with," I said.

On cue, there was a knock on the entrance door. Stella hurried out, returning in a moment with Teddy's grandparents. Although I felt confident with Stella here, my insides churned like a wobbly wheel. I kept my hands clasped tightly together. After we got through introductions, Stella launched into the outlines of the meeting while I studied Teddy's parents.

Paul's mother was petite with curly salt and pepper hair, glasses, and a warm smile. His father was all gray, tall, and thin with a serious expression. About halfway through, I almost backed out of telling them the whole truth, but I wanted them to understand why I was so distrustful of their son. Part of me kept thinking that maybe it didn't matter in the long run, but I knew that it did. Paul was a liar in a sneaky way, and he could create more problems in the future.

After I stumbled through my halting explanation, I twisted my hands together under the table and looked over them. His mother was quiet for a few beats before her lips pressed together as she shook her head sharply. "I am *so* sorry."

Paul's father closed his eyes and leaned his head back for a moment. The whole thing was so embarrassing and I was still so ashamed. I'd never imagined myself explaining to strangers about their son taking a condom off in the middle of sex. It was horribly embarrassing.

When Paul's father brought his gaze to mine, I wasn't sure what I saw there, but I thought it was disappointment mingled with anger. "Paul is selfish. He takes care of himself. This isn't the first time this happened," he said.

"You have another grandchild?" My voice rose up sharply at the end.

His mother shook her head. "No. She didn't get pregnant, but she pressed charges. That was in California where it's illegal."

"Oh," was my single word reply. I glanced to Stella, uncertain of what to do with this turn in the conversation.

Stella's sharp eyes arced around the table. "So, Paul's behavior isn't a surprise?"

Paul's mother looked down at the table. When her gaze lifted again, pain shimmered there. "We didn't know that's what happened here." She paused before flattening her palms on the table, as if steeling herself. "Are you glad you had...?"

When her words trailed off, I interjected quickly, "Absolutely. I don't regret having Teddy for a millisecond. I don't like how it happened. I certainly didn't plan on getting pregnant and having a baby. But the way it happened has most definitely affected my trust in Paul. It's my understanding from what he said that he doesn't really want any involvement."

Paul's father finally spoke, "Of course he doesn't. Responsibility isn't something he's interested in. We wish we could understand, but clearly, we didn't instill a strong moral compass in him."

What I said next was impulsive, but for some reason, I trusted them. "I'm definitely not opposed to your involvement. I'm willing for you to have visits as long as you respect my boundaries with Paul. Maybe someday he'll change his mind. Maybe he'll demonstrate he can be responsible and trustworthy in the future, but right now, it's important to me that you respect that I don't want him to be involved. I don't even want child support from him."

"We completely understand," his mother replied. "We've already discussed it with our attorney. We're willing to do supervised visits, to visit only in locations where you're comfortable, with whatever guidelines you want to set. We would love to have a relationship with our grandson. We don't really understand why Paul does the things he does, and maybe it's partly our fault."

I glanced toward Stella, because I knew my emotions might get in the way here. I picked up the black pen.

She jumped right in. "This meeting was for both parties to get a sense of how to move forward. We've already drawn up a visitation agreement. To start, it does involve only visits in public locations and those will be time-limited."

I was beyond grateful for Stella. She deftly kept the

conversation rolling over the next few minutes. We even scheduled a time for them to officially meet Teddy. After they left, I threw my arms around her, the intensity of my own relief overwhelming me.

She smiled when I finally released her. "So you feel okay?"

"Thanks to you and Colin. I can't tell you how much I appreciate you being here today." I paused and took a shaky breath, trying to compose myself. "So what do we do about Paul now?"

"Colin will follow up with his attorney. At this point, it doesn't seem like we need to be concerned about demands from him with regard to his parents. I'll keep you looped in on any updates. You just go about your day now."

I left, feeling a sense of lightness gusting through me like a soft breeze. The stress I'd been carrying had felt so heavy for weeks now. I wanted to see Griffin so much. I shot off a quick text.

Me: *I'd love to see you.*

Chapter Forty

TISH

I was almost done for the day and was busy checking email on my laptop when my cell phone rang. I should've thought to check who was calling, but I was feeling more relaxed. My guard was down after finally dealing with the stress of the last few weeks.

"Hi, it's Tish," I answered.

"Fucking bitch," Paul opened with.

"Paul?" My heart started to pound in a rapid, sickly beat.

"Yeah. Why did you tell my parents that?"

"Because I don't trust you. I'm not asking for anything from you. No child support, no visits, nothing."

"You fucked me over, Tish."

Just as I was about to end the call, the line clicked. Restless, I stood from my desk. I needed some water. I started to cross my office, but I should've known better. My blood pressure began to plummet and I stumbled. I reached for my desk just as my knees gave out. I distantly heard something falling with me.

I had no idea how much time I was out, but it

must've been a few minutes. When I dragged my eyes open, Archer was kneeling in front of me, telling someone, "I've already called 911. I have no idea what happened. I heard something fall and then a thump. I came in and she was unconscious. Oh wait, her eyes are opening. Tish? Are you okay?" He waved his hand in front of my face.

"I'm fine, Archer." I straightened slightly. I'd fallen at an awkward angle.

"She says she's fine," he said.

"Who are you talking to?" I mumbled.

"Griffin. He's on his way over with whoever's coming from the station."

"Oh, my God, you turned this into a whole drama," I muttered. I started to move, but my foot slipped out from under me on the carpeting, and I fell against my desk again.

Chapter Forty-One

GRIFFIN

Tish sat across from me, alternating her glare between Archer and me.

Adrenaline was still pumping through me. I knew she was safe, but Archer's call had sent fear skyrocketing through me. She sat before me, looking seriously annoyed.

"You could have told me this is something that happens to you sometimes," Archer was saying. "Forgive me for getting stressed out when you passed out."

Poor Archer appeared genuinely flummoxed by Tish's obvious annoyance with him. "It's not a big deal. You don't need to worry about it. In fact, it's in my HR file. I have syncope episodes, which basically means sometimes I faint. That's it."

"I don't look through employee's HR paperwork!" Archer protested just as Phoebe came walking into Tish's office.

She looked from Tish, to Archer, to me, and back to Archer. "Is everything okay?" She stopped beside Archer, resting her hand on his shoulder and giving him a reassuring squeeze.

"Tish fainted," Archer explained. "Apparently, this is something she's prone to, and she's pissed off because I called 911. Dana is here to clear her."

Dana from the EMT crew smiled amongst us. "Griffin can't be the official responder because, well, he's not objective."

"I'm objective!" I protested.

Phoebe gave me what I could only describe as a pitying look. "You don't even realize you're head over heels in love with Tish. I'm sure you could rescue her and everything would be fine, but let Dana handle this."

I heard myself breathe loudly through my nose and felt like a horse pawing at the ground.

Tish came to my defense. "Griffin can handle anything." Her cheeks flushed deep pink when she caught my eyes, and I wanted to kiss her. I'd missed her, so fucking much.

Now that I was sure she was okay, I wanted her all to myself. I would take even one minute with her all to myself. Instead, I had my cousin, his wife, and then Chase who appeared in the doorway, glancing around at the tableau of people crowded into Tish's office.

"Everything okay?" he asked.

Dana stood, hefting her bag onto her shoulder. "Everything is fine." Her gaze whisked around the room before landing on Tish. "I think everybody but Griffin needs to come with me."

"Why?" Chase prompted. He had no fucking clue what was happening.

"Because I said so. I'm the lead EMT for the moment, so consider me in charge until you're all out of this office," she replied.

Dana briskly ushered the group out of the office,

leaving me alone with Tish when the door clicked shut behind everyone.

Tish's eyes locked to mine. There were so many things I wanted to say, but all that came out was, "I love you."

She blinked before bursting into tears.

In a millisecond, I was kneeling on the floor in front of her and wrapping her in my arms. She tucked her face into the curve of my neck and took several shuddery breaths.

When she lifted her head, I kept one arm curled around her waist and smoothed a loose lock of hair off her cheek. "This feels big and dramatic, and I've had a stressful day. I love you," she said with a sniffle.

It felt like my heart was smiling. "I know Archer didn't need to call 911, but I'm glad he did."

"I just feel so stupid." She rolled her eyes and leaned back in her chair a little. I let my arm slide away, my hands falling to rest on her hips. "I faint and people think it's a big deal and it's just this dumb syncope disorder. And, you always seem to show up."

"What happened today?"

She twisted her hands together in her lap. "I met Teddy's grandparents. Ever since Paul showed up—" Her breath came out in a huff. "Colin has been amazing. His paralegal Stella helped me with everything. Paul's an asshole, but his parents seem really nice. I told them what he did. When I got back here, Paul called me and he's furious. I fainted when I got up to get something to eat."

"I'd like to kick Paul's ass," I said bluntly.

"Please don't. I appreciate that you want to. Maybe I didn't need to take space from you to handle this, but it's what I needed to think. Thank you for giving me that time."

I held her gaze, my heart pounding along in my chest at a fast clip. "I didn't like it, but I understand."

Tish blinked before leaning forward and giving me a kiss. It was brief, just a soft brushing of her lips across mine before she leaned back again. My heart felt pulled forward, as if the invisible threads between us were drawing tighter.

"Let's go home," she whispered.

Chapter Forty-Two

TISH

That evening, I experienced a mix of emotions. I was deeply relieved Griffin was home with me and Teddy. I was still unsettled by the call from Paul. Even though I felt comfortable moving forward with visits with Teddy's grandparents, it had drained me emotionally to deal with them today. Somehow, Griffin knew exactly what I needed.

I was a little sheepish about the state of my house. With me working again and Griffin gone recently, it was a little messier than I liked. As soon as we got home, he helped me get Teddy settled in the playpen and began tidying up in the kitchen while I organized the living room and bedroom. He even offered to make dinner.

"You're doing too much!" I protested.

"I'm not, Tish." He swept his hand in an arc. "All I did was wash the dishes."

My cheeks heated. "Fine. We could order takeout."

He waggled his brows. "Or, I could make mac and cheese."

I snorted. "Let's get something delivered. We can do the Gallery Café or Alpenglow Pizza. Your pick."

"Speaking of delivery, when is the brewery here going to start offering takeout in town?" he asked.

"I don't know exactly. They have the brewery almost ready, and Archer and Chase have mostly been focusing on getting the distribution center going here. The restaurant is scheduled to be fully operational by next summer," I explained.

Griffin nodded. "So, what do you want for food tonight? That's the pertinent question."

"You pick," I replied.

"Let's do the Gallery Café."

Hours later, after we'd had dinner and Teddy was asleep, Griffin made lingering love to me. After driving me beyond the edge with his fingers and his mouth, I savored the feel of his weight coming over me when he stretched my arms above my head.

His gaze held mine, dark and intent, as he filled me in a slow slide. "Can you come for me? Just once more, sweetness?" he whispered in my ear.

I was caught in a haze of need, almost drunk with pleasure. "Yes," I gasped when he drew back and thrust forward.

We flew together moments later, and he held me close as we fell asleep.

A few days later, I met Stella at the office to review the updated agreement. Blessedly, there hadn't been another phone call from Paul.

Stella waited patiently, her hands folded together on the conference table. "Colin says everything should be all set after we finalize this."

After I reviewed everything and signed, I glanced over. "Any updates on Paul from Colin? I don't want to ask, but he was so angry in his last call that I was worried."

"Colin has spoken with his attorney and advised we'll file a protective order if he does anything like that again. My understanding is his parents have also spoken with him," she explained.

"Should I be worried?" As if I could stop worrying. I internally rolled my eyes.

Stella twisted her lips to the side. "I'd like to say no. But family cases tend to be messy. I don't think you need to worry about him getting custody, and he certainly doesn't seem interested in visitation, but it doesn't mean that he can't make things uncomfortable for you."

"That's what I'm worried about."

"Please reach out if anything comes up at all. We can handle it," she assured me.

"I hope so." I was just about to leave when I remembered to check on payment. "Where are we with the billing? I know it's adding up, so I'd like to maybe set up a payment plan." I hated worrying about money, but attorneys were the opposite of cheap.

Stella slid her laptop closer. A few clicks later, she glanced up. "You're fully paid."

"Huh? Are you sure?"

She nodded. "Positive."

"Can you call Colin? There must be a mistake."

A moment later, she had him on speaker. "What can I do for you?" Colin asked.

"Colin, Stella's saying there's no payment due. That doesn't make sense," I said.

"Griffin took care of it just this morning."

"Excuse me?"

"Just what I said."

My cheeks were on fire and I felt mortified. Obviously, I appreciated Griffin's intentions, but I needed to do this myself.

I tried to sound calm as I thanked Colin. Stella and I walked out together. With Stella's office beside Firehouse Café, the parking lot was visible from here. When I glanced over, I saw Griffin standing beside his truck. Without thinking, I immediately veered in that direction.

"Griffin! You could've at least told me you were going to do that." I stopped in front of him a minute later.

"Tish!" I heard Stella's voice but ignored it. "You left your keys!"

I stayed focused on Griffin. "Tell you what?" he asked.

Griffin was standing beside another man who I'd seen before, but didn't know. He looked from me to Griffin. "You must be Tish," he said with a smile.

I gave him a distracted glance. "Nice to meet you."

Stella caught up to me. "Here." She thrust my keys at me.

I reached for them and promptly dropped them on the ground. Griffin leaned over to scoop them up.

"Here you go." It annoyed me that the subtle brush of his fingers against mine sent sparks in a hot scatter through me when he handed over my keys.

"Is everything okay?" Stella asked next. "You ran off pretty quick there."

My gaze whisked around the small circle, and I let out a sigh. We officially had an audience and I didn't want to get into my embarrassment about the bill. "Have you met Griffin?" I asked Stella. "If not, this is Griffin Cannon. And—"

"Hudson," Griffin filled in. "Hudson, this is Tish and Stella." His gaze paused on Stella. "Nice to meet you."

Hudson smiled between us. "Nice to meet both of you. Griffin missed you, by the way."

When Hudson looked at Stella, I didn't miss the flare of appreciation in his eyes. Stella was adorably cute and sexy, so I didn't blame him one bit. She smiled up at him. "Are you a firefighter too?"

"Yes ma'am," he drawled.

"Seems like there's a lot of those around here," she said.

As if on cue, an actual firetruck pulled up on the street and several firefighters piled out.

Griffin glanced at me and nudged his head to the side. "What is it?" he asked once we were out of earshot beside his truck, while Stella and Hudson were talking with the other firefighters who had just arrived.

"You could've told me you were going to pay my bill. I can take care of it," I ground out.

He was quiet for several beats. "Tish, I just wanted to help. I should've told you."

I chewed the inside of one cheek as I studied him. "Thank you."

"I guess maybe I need not to rush into things. I planned to mention it tonight."

Trying to keep my annoyance in check, I shrugged. "Just talk to me when you're feeling that helpful."

"I will." He startled me by dipping his head and giving me a fierce kiss. Enough so that when we broke apart, my cheeks were on fire and I was hot all over.

Somebody nearby let out a whistle and I glanced over. Griffin reached for my hand as he glanced over. "Really, Beck," he said dryly.

Chapter Forty-Three

TISH

My annoyance about Griffin's high-handedness was still chafing at me when he called me that afternoon. I was tied up with a meeting at work and didn't get a chance to take his call. Roughly an hour later, I learned his crew had gotten called out to another fire. My annoyance disappeared as quickly as a balloon popping.

A near-instant worry rose inside. I tried to call him back, but he didn't answer. I hurried down the hallway to search for Phoebe.

"What is it?" she asked when I walked into her office.

"Griffin's crew got called out to a fire."

Her gaze was warm and sympathetic, and she pulled me into a quick hug.

"Why did I have to fall in love with a firefighter?" I bemoaned.

Phoebe squeezed my shoulders before she stepped back. "You did, so you'll learn to deal with it."

Phoebe insisted I come with her to card night.

With everything going on, I had forgotten about it. A serious side effect of having a baby all by myself was I had become wildly forgetful.

Conveniently, Madison was hosting, so I didn't even have to go out of my way to get there. When I arrived with Phoebe, Allie immediately swept Teddy into her arms. Maisie came in with Lucy and Amelia on her heels. Holly, Tiffany, and Farrah joined us, along with Susannah and Jasmine.

It was always a mix-and-match group, and I was pleasantly surprised to see Stella there. She smiled at me when I sat down beside her. "I'm so glad you're here!"

"I was at Firehouse Café, and, Janet introduced me to Maisie. She invited me," Stella explained. "I'm new here, so thought it'd be good to get to know some people."

I smiled around at my newfound friends before my gaze made its way back to Stella. "I'm still new to town, but they make me feel like I belong."

Madison sat down on my other side, curling her arm around my shoulders and squeezing tight before leaning back. "Of course you belong."

While we were nibbling on an array of appetizers, we began a casual game of cards and the usual chatter started. During a pause, Phoebe piped up, "Tish is learning that dating a firefighter can be stressful."

I felt my cheeks get hot when all eyes turned to me. "Griffin and Graham's crew got called out," Madison explained.

"I promise you'll get used to it," Amelia chimed in.

Maisie nodded vigorously. "Of course I worry about Beck when he's gone and I miss him like crazy. Aside from the worry, there are perks. I get plenty of my own time and hot welcome-home sex."

Stella snorted. "Is that what we're calling it?"

"Well, it's not make-up sex, and I think it's better," Maisie replied matter-of-factly.

"So, how serious are you and Griffin?" Susannah asked.

"Pretty serious, I think."

"Do you love him?" Maisie pressed.

I slid my gaze to her. Amelia let out a dry chuckle. "Beck is the nosy guy, and Maisie is the nosy girl."

"I call it curious," Maisie said. "You don't have to answer."

"I don't mind. I do love him. I just can't believe he even wants to be with me. I have a baby, and it's not his baby, and then this whole drama happened..." I threw a hand up in the air.

That led to plenty of questions and I had to fill everyone in on the events around Paul and his parents. Stella mostly stayed quiet.

"You work at the law firm, are you helping her with this?" Farrah asked.

Stella held her palms up. "I can't talk about it unless Tish wants to."

"Stella has been amazing. It's all good. I just hope Paul doesn't do anything else shitty," I added.

"If he does, we'll kick his ass," Tiffany said.

As my gaze encircled the table, my heart felt full. When I moved to Willow Brook, I'd been feeling lost. My lifeline had been my job, but I'd been beyond startled to find myself unexpectedly pregnant and struggling with the way it had come about. Because of these women, I felt like I belonged somewhere, like they had my back.

"I know you would, but I think it'll be okay," I replied.

The night moved along with plenty of laughter and

more lighthearted gossip. By the time the group started to filter apart, multiple phones vibrated, rang, or chimed all within seconds of each other. An evening that felt good and embracing took a sharp turn.

Maisie got the full story the fastest. While she wasn't on duty tonight, she had the dispatcher at the station on speed dial.

"The engine went out on one of the planes." Her gaze was steady, but I could see the worry flickering. "Nate was able to bring the plane down, but they're in an area where there's no cell reception. They radioed in. Everyone survived, but that's all we know."

Of those of us here, Madison, Farrah, Tiffany, and I all had firefighters we loved on that plane, and Holly's husband was the pilot. For the next half an hour, we were locked in a pattern of making calls and trying to gather more information until Maisie finally looked around the group. "We're not going to get any more information until the rescue group is able to reach the site."

Madison glanced around, her expression stoic. "Everyone is welcome to stay, but I know we all deal with things like this differently. This is a waiting game at this point."

Over the following hour, most of the group left with everyone planning to stay in close contact.

Holly looked sick, her normally sunny expression shuttered with her eyes puffy and mascara streaked on her cheeks. "I don't even want to call Nate's parents."

"You know they're going to find out," Madison said.

Holly blew a puff of air out, expertly dislodging a loose lock of hair falling in front of her eyes. "You're right. I'll just go over there. Are you sure you're okay?"

The group had dwindled to Madison, Allie, me, and Phoebe. Phoebe had called Archer and told him she wanted to stay with me until we had some news. This used to be Phoebe's crew.

"Go to his parents," I said. "Maisie said she's going to call as soon as she hears anything."

The frustration that had boiled over this morning about Griffin paying for my attorney felt so insignificant now. I just wanted him home.

Allie looked absolutely distraught with worry about her father. She coped by focusing on Teddy and her little brother, Harry, who was two years old now. Madison made coffee and we sat around the living room with the TV on in a rumble in the background.

Madison's cell phone vibrated. She had it on speaker before a second ring could happen. "What's the update?" she asked.

"They're on-site and I don't have any updates on who, there are some injuries, but everyone is expected to survive," Maisie said quickly.

"Is there any way we can talk to any of them?" My voice cracked at the end as tears rolled down my cheeks.

"I wish," Maisie said. "I *really* do. They're communicating through radio only and that's limited to the rescue crew."

"Do we have a time frame?" Madison asked.

Allie had returned to the living room. She sank her hips slowly onto the couch beside Madison, leaning into her as Madison curled her arm around Allie's shoulders.

"Best guess is they can get back in maybe six hours or so. Even though the wait is hard, everyone is alive and okay," Maisie said.

I hated the waiting. I wanted Griffin here. Home. With me.

I was too restless to leave, knowing that if I went home, I would pace by myself with my thoughts gamboling around in my brain. We collectively decided to wait out the night.

Chapter Forty-Four

GRIFFIN

"How ya holding up?" I asked.

Hudson rolled his head to the side and shrugged. "Been better, but I'm okay."

Nate let out a dry chuckle. "I think we've all been better. We could also be worse."

"You landed the plane about as perfectly as possible under the circumstances," I said to Nate.

Nate was one of the pilots who contracted to fly hotshot crews all over Alaska. He'd been flying half of our twenty-five-member crew out to this fire when one of the engines on the plane had gone out. It was fairly common, even for commercial flights, for birds to get sucked into engines. We assumed that's what had happened.

"I'm just damn glad we were in a larger plane with two engines," Nate commented.

Single-engine planes crisscrossed the skies of Alaska by the hundreds on a daily basis. When the engine had gone out, Nate had expertly navigated as the plane drifted lower. Fortunately for all of us, we hadn't yet reached the more mountainous region. We could see the smoke from the fire he'd been trying to bring us to.

Of the twelve of us on this plane, we were mostly a little banged up with a few injuries more serious here and there. One of the wings had clipped some trees on the way down. Hudson appeared to have taken the worst of it. Considering that all of us were trained in emergency first responder wilderness first aid, we quickly assessed the situation. I was pretty sure I had a broken collarbone but I was otherwise okay.

Bruising was forming on Nate's shoulder from where a branch came through the window and clipped him hard. Hudson had been seated beside the wing that hit the trees and his knee was swelling badly. So far, he was turning down any suggestions for pain medication stronger than ibuprofen.

Aside from my broken collarbone, Tate Halston had a nasty gash in his side from the tree branch coming through his window. We would all be sore from the impact. Considering the dangers of flying in Alaska's backcountry and thanks to Nate's skilled landing, we were lucky. We also had just enough daylight left for the landing. We knew we'd likely be spending the night out here.

The plane's radio crackled and Nate hurried over. A moment later, he returned to the group, reporting, "Looks like they should be here within a few hours. They're sending two helicopters."

As hotshot firefighters, we were prepared to spend the night out here. We had first aid, equipment, food, and the gear we needed to comfortably survive in the wilderness for up to two weeks, but trying to tough it out with injuries wasn't pleasant.

We'd made ourselves as comfortable as possible and were resting on our gear packs. We were passing around snacks, and Graham had even broken out a pack of cards.

"Will they keep the other half of the crew out at the fire?" I asked.

"Probably to start, but they'll send another full crew out," Graham replied.

While we waited, my mind kept spinning to Tish. During my last trip out, I had missed her. A lot. The shock of our unexpected crash landing made the ache of missing her acute. For the first time since I'd become a hotshot firefighter, I could see the end of my shelf life in this career.

I glanced toward Nate. "Being a pilot's not a bad gig," I pointed out. "Do you miss Holly when you fly away?"

"Of course. But I don't have to be gone too long," he pointed out.

Graham chuckled as he played a card in the game of rummy he was playing with Jonah, Hudson, and Wes.

"Statistically speaking, what Nate does is more dangerous than what we do," Jonah pointed out.

"How long do you think you'll be doing this?" I asked Graham.

He smiled quickly, his gaze understanding and bemused. "Are you contemplating your life choices now that you're in love with Tish?"

I shrugged. "I guess I am. I always knew there was an expiration date to being a firefighter. The physical demands are hard."

"Absolutely," Jonah offered up as Graham and Wes nodded in agreement.

"I love my job," Graham added. "I always miss Madison and Allie when I'm away. Aside from the risk, oddly, I think it makes our marriage better."

"Seriously?" I prompted.

Jonah chimed in, "It may sound strange, but yes. I guess it gives you perspective on what matters. I don't let the little things get in the way."

"I don't have a time frame, but maybe a few more years," Wes said. "Unless, of course, an injury takes me out."

Hudson shifted, glancing amongst us. "I'm short on relationship advice, but I figure this job is stupid after a decade," he offered.

A laugh rustled in my throat. "I don't have a time frame yet, but being with Tish makes me wonder about it. When will they report the crash to the station in Willow Brook?" I glanced toward Graham.

"I'm sure they already have. Maisie'll get the scoop and pass on the updates," Graham said.

My heart squeezed. "Tish is going to be worried."

"They'll all be worried, but they'll also know we're okay," Jonah said.

"Do you think they'll take us to Willow Brook when they pick us up?" I asked.

"Probably," Wes said. "It's the closest hospital. Anchorage is nearby, but none of us have serious enough injuries to worry about going there."

The following hours were a blur of waiting and ignoring the achy pain of my collarbone. Fortunately, although darkness fell, the weather stayed clear. Within a few hours, a helicopter was carrying us to Willow Brook.

Once we were in the air, my impatience to see Tish ramped up. The feeling of missing her was sharp. I was anxious to explain to her that I hadn't meant to frustrate her by covering her legal bill. In hindsight, I realized that it must have come across as high-handed.

Every situation was different, but I was learning intention didn't always matter. Especially not when it involved someone else's life.

I wanted to call Tish as soon as we got back into range for calls, but my phone had cracked badly during the crash landing and wasn't working.

Nate glanced over as we got closer. "I'm calling Holly. Do you want me to see if she can track Tish down?"

"Please."

Chapter Forty-Five

TISH

"Hurry," I said to Holly.

"I'm hurrying," she insisted.

After a fitful few hours of sleep on Madison's couch, I woke to Holly knocking on the door before the sun was even up. She shared the update from Maisie. According to Maisie's information, Nate, Graham, and Griffin, along with a few of the other firefighters, were on the first helicopter and would be taken straight to the hospital to be cleared.

Moments later, Holly was practically skidding into the parking lot at the hospital. We flew through the doors, and Holly had all the information within minutes. She wasn't on duty, but she was a supervisor for the nurse's team here in the ER. She knew exactly who to find to get the quickest update.

Although there were only a few minor injuries for those on the plane, Griffin had broken his collarbone. All I wanted was to be able to see him. It felt like forever before we got any more information.

A nurse came out and gestured for me to follow

him down the hallway. "I'm Chris. Come on back. He's doing well."

I bolted across the room to his side.

"Do you want me to come in with you?" Chris asked as we stood at the doorway a few minutes later.

I took a shaky breath. "I think I can handle it." I was already on the verge of tears and had been for hours. Even though I knew Griffin was okay, I was desperate to see him.

Chris gave me an encouraging smile. "Just use the call button in there if he needs anything." With a light squeeze on my shoulder, he hurried down the hallway.

I opened the door, standing there with my palm pressed to my chest through several echoing beats of my heart. Griffin was sitting in a chair with his arm in a sling. After being frozen for a moment, I rushed over. His eyes lifted to mine as he stood quickly, wrapping me in an embrace with one arm. "I'm fine," he murmured into my hair.

"Oh, my God, I've been so worried," I mumbled into his chest before leaning back to look up into his eyes.

"I'm fine," he repeated.

I took a shaky breath. "I feel like I've been waiting forever. Are you sure you're okay?" I ran my hands over his chest and back. He was wearing a pair of hospital scrubs.

"How's your collarbone?" I stepped back, carefully sliding a palm down his upper arm.

He shrugged. "Fine." His eyes held mine. "I love you." His voice was low and a little ragged.

I burst into tears, hiccupping as I said, "I love you too. I'm sorry I got upset about the payment thing." I gestured vaguely in the air.

"I should've talked to you about it. I wanted to help, but I understand why you were upset."

"And, you did help. You really did. Are you sure you're okay?" I repeated.

"I am absolutely okay. I have to wear a sling for a while and be careful, but that's it. They said it could be up to six weeks, but should be less."

"When can you leave the hospital?"

"Whenever they set me free."

Just then, there was a light knock at the door. I glanced over my shoulder as Griffin called out, "Come in!"

The nurse peered around the door as he opened it. "You are cleared for discharge." Chris waggled his brows as he smiled.

A breath I hadn't even known I was holding whooshed out.

"Where's Teddy?" Griffin asked a few minutes later as he was signing paperwork to discharge.

"Allie still has him. When we found out what happened, we were at Madison's. Maisie kept us up to date. Everyone else is okay, right?'

Griffin nodded. "Hudson's knee got dislocated. A few others were banged up from the crash landing. Nate pulled off a damn miracle when that engine went out."

I still had my arm curled around his waist and turned my head to press a kiss on his good shoulder.

A short while later, we were back at the house. As soon as Teddy saw Griffin, he let out a squeal of joy. When I walked back into the living room to find Griffin settled onto the couch and Teddy playing with his toys on the floor, my heart cartwheeled. *This* was home. It wasn't a place. It was *us*.

EPILOGUE

Hudson Fox

Four months later

I reached for my crutches, silently cursing as I pulled them out of my truck. Walking with crutches meant a slow hobble into Fireweed Winery. My friends Griffin and Tish were having a gathering here to celebrate their recent engagement.

I rested my crutches against the back of my truck. Conveniently, I could drive because my left knee was the problem. I ignored it when my crutches toppled over to the ground.

When I discovered I'd forgotten my wallet, I carefully hobbled to the driver's side door to fetch it out of the console between the seats. Just as I closed the door, I heard the sound of tires on gravel and glanced up to see a hatchback car approaching.

My eyes snagged on tumbled blond curls just as there was a loud crunching sound and the car came to a jerking stop. I reached the back of my truck and looked down to see my crutches crumpled under a front tire.

The woman who was driving leapt out, her eyes going wide when she looked down. "Oh, my God! I didn't see them! I am *so* sorry."

I'd seen this woman before. Stella. She was impossible to forget. My hormones had emblazoned her in bold strokes into my memory. Her glossy blond curls bounced as she looked between me and my crumpled crutches.

Stella met my gaze, her brown eyes wide. "Hudson? Right?"

I smiled. "That's right. Nice to see you again, Stella."

"Oh, my gosh! You got injured in the plane crash."

"Right on two counts," I said with a chuckle. "Don't worry, I can get a new pair of crutches. To be honest, I hate them. Using them gets old fast."

Stella pressed a palm to her chest. She looked distraught.

"Stella, it's no big deal. I can still drive. I'll just hobble around this afternoon."

"I know, but..."

I hopped closer to the back of my truck as Stella bent down and fetched my bent crutches.

I reached for the one that looked less bent. "This will work."

She looked at it doubtfully. I took the other one from her and tossed it in the back of my truck cab.

"I'll walk you in," she said, holding out her elbow.

"I appreciate it, but you should probably park your car first," I pointed out.

"Oh!" She hurried around the front of her car.

She quickly parked on the other side of my truck and climbed out. I didn't need her to walk in me, but I certainly wouldn't mind it. She was cute as hell, and the spark I felt just looking at her burned bright and hot.

She stopped beside me, tucking her keys in her purse before holding her elbow out again.

My lips tugged into a smile. Stella was easily a foot shorter than me. "I appreciate that, but it'll be lopsided. Why don't you just walk beside me?"

Her curls swung with her vigorous nod. She insisted on staying at my side as I began to awkwardly hop along on the one crutch. I contemplated going without it altogether, but I really wasn't supposed to put much weight on that knee yet.

"I know there was a crash landing and a couple of the firefighters were injured, but what happened to your knee?" she asked as we walked.

"I dislocated it. It was almost better, but then I dislocated it again." I rolled my eyes. My own impatience had created that issue.

"I bet that hurt," she commented.

"Ten-ten would not recommend," I said dryly.

All things considered, it could've been much worse. When an engine went out, the pilot had executed a controlled crash landing. One of the wings hit some trees, and I dislocated my knee somehow. It's one of those injuries that's not horrible, but annoying as hell.

"How did you dislocate it the second time?" Stella peered up at me, her teeth catching the plump pink surface of her bottom lip. The sight of it jolted me with a hot sizzle.

She seemed oblivious to her effect on me. I ordered my hormones to stand down. With only one hand available, I couldn't risk trying to adjust my jeans as I felt a subtle swelling against my zipper.

"I was letting my cat out on the porch and I tripped."

"Oh," Stella replied slowly.

My eyes focused on her lips forming the shape of that single word. She had freckled cheeks and big brown eyes. She was on the short side with enough curves that the buttons on her blouse were strained. She was wearing a skirt that fell to her knees and flared out with a little ruffle, paired with a button-down blouse and fitted leather boots. Her clothes hugged her close, delineating every curve. It was distracting as hell.

When we approached the doorway to the winery, she hurried ahead, her hips swinging with every step. She held the door open, smiling as she gestured me through. "I'm assuming you're here for the engagement party too?"

"Sure am."

I glanced around once we walked inside. So far, this place was only used for events. Fireweed Winery was well-known in Alaska. It was an international brewery and distributor now, and it had all started in Alaska. Griffin Cannon, a fellow firefighter, and my friend, had family who ran the corporation.

The location was beautiful. They'd renovated an old plane hangar. High beams crisscrossed the ceiling above. They'd kept the industrial look but softened it with color and wooden touches. The floor was stained to a deep mahogany shade. Brightly colored rugs were scattered about the space. There was a small circular bar in the center, along with a bar running the full length of one side.

The back wall had windows floor to ceiling, offering a beautiful view out over a nearby lake. There were tables scattered throughout the area. Stella herded me over to one, insisting on pulling out a chair for me.

Just as I was resting my bent crutch against the table, Griffin and Tish approached. Griffin's eyes landed on the crutch. "What the hell happened?"

Before I could respond, Stella jumped in, "I didn't see his crutches on the ground and I drove over them. This one's in the best shape." She grimaced, glancing down to me apologetically. "I really am sorry. I will buy you a new pair of crutches. I'd do it right now, but I don't know where to get them."

Tish smiled between us, her eyes twinkling. "Hudson looks okay."

I gave a thumbs-up. "I am."

"I thought your knee was better," Tish added.

"He tripped when he let his cat out," Griffin explained with a chuckle.

Tish snorted. "Really?"

"Yeah, I love my cat," I countered.

"Stella is one of the most efficient human beings I've ever known, so I'm sure she can figure out where to get those crutches for you by tomorrow," Tish said.

"If you tell me where, I could go now," Stella interjected.

I shook my head. "No need. I got them from my doctor's office." I glanced around the room to see Charlie Franklin, the doctor in question, with her husband. In the small-town world of Willow Brook, my doctor was married to another hotshot firefighter, Jesse Franklin. "I know her office is closed today because she's right over there."

Stella moved as if she was going to walk over there. I reached out and caught her hand in mine. At the mere touch of her, electricity sizzled up my arm.

"It's really okay. I'll give her office a call tomorrow. The receptionist will take care of it."

Griffin chuckled as he glanced toward Stella. "Hudson's fine, you don't need to worry. We have plenty of food and drinks. I will go order–" he began just as a waiter stopped by our table.

Tish elbowed Griffin in the side. "Let them do their jobs."

The waiter took our orders and moved along. Griffin and Tish sat down with us, along with a few other firefighters and friends.

"This is a really nice space," I commented to Griffin.

"Thank you. I'd like to take credit, but Chase and Archer have been coordinating this part, along with the restaurant manager back in Fireweed Harbor. Tish is running the whole show on the admin side."

Tish rolled her eyes. "I manage the office here for Fireweed Industries, but I haven't really done much for this project, except tell them when I thought things looked good and take care of paperwork."

"I am so glad the winery added a location here," Stella chimed in. "That's part of the reason why the law office where I work added a location here. As soon as I finish up my law degree, I'll be able to start here."

Stella's eyes twinkled with her smile. My eyes lingered on the little dimple that peeked out.

STELLA

The table was crowded, and I scooted my chair over to make room for someone else. My leg bumped into Hudson's and I jumped. "Oh, God! Is that your bad knee?" Not thinking, I actually put my hand on his thigh.

Hudson slid his gaze to mine, his green eyes darkening. "No, but you can leave your hand there," he teased.

Hudson had this low, raspy voice that made my belly spin in flips and my hormones twirl. I couldn't help but laugh as I took my hand away.

I cleared my throat, willing the heat rising in my cheeks to dissipate. I knew it wouldn't. I was prone to blushing.

"How is your knee?" I asked.

"It's getting better. I've been very careful." He patted the knee on his opposite side. "So, if I trip again, hopefully it'll be okay."

I cleared my throat again because I couldn't think of what to say. "I hope it's all better soon," I finally said.

There were plenty of lighthearted jokes about Hudson's bent crutch. At one point, his doctor came over. She was pretty with dark hair and almost-violet eyes. "Tell me what happened?" She eyed the crutch resting beside him.

"It's my fault!" I actually raised my hand as if I was in class.

Hudson chuckled as his gaze slid toward me. My belly felt all funny when his eyes met mine. He was *way* too good-looking with rumpled brown curls and green eyes. Although he had an easy manner to him, there was an intensity shimmering underneath. I sensed he had secrets, and, oh, boy, did I love a man with secrets. My hormones *loved* a mysterious man.

When his doctor prompted, "Oh?" I added, "I drove over them because I didn't see them."

The doctor smiled. "Ah, well, Hudson will be fine. I'm Charlie Franklin, by the way."

"Stella Lancaster," I replied. "Nice to meet you."

"Technically, in the chain of events, the crutches fell first, so it's not really your fault," Hudson offered with a low laugh.

Charlie assured me I could stop by the office to get him a new set of crutches the next day. As the gathering carried on, I got to hold Tish's adorable little baby boy, Teddy. Teddy had plump cheeks and a sweet giggle. Eventually, it was time for the purpose of this party. I held Teddy while Griffin's twin brother made a toast.

"Griffin, the last," Wyatt said, holding a glass of wine aloft.

Griffin chuckled. They had a big family, and the oldest brother also made a toast, offering, "It's the scandal that never was. Griffin still doesn't work for the family yet, so..." Rhys grinned over at Griffin and Tish.

Her cheeks were pink as she looked up at Griffin. Even though there were about forty people here, it almost seemed as if they were entirely alone. The look in Griffin's eyes was filled with love.

For just a minute, my little wishful heart wondered if maybe I could have something like that. My cynical mind elbowed its way in. *Not so fast. You know that whenever you hope for something like that, it doesn't work out.*

I had a terrible tendency to fall for guys who treated me like an afterthought. I was a perpetual people pleaser, even for people I shouldn't worry about pleasing.

I bounced Teddy in my arms and kept my focus on my happiness for my friends. I eventually threaded my way through the well-wishers to hand Teddy back to Tish when she waved me over. "Here's your little guy."

"Thank you so much for holding him," Tish said as

Griffin reached for Teddy. Teddy squealed, kicking his feet in joy.

I'd gotten to know Tish because I'd been the paralegal helping on her custody case. Blessedly, that was all resolved.

When I returned to the table to fetch my purse and keys, Hudson was standing there with his bent crutch. My belly did another little shimmy. When he looked up and caught my eyes, my lungs seized, and heat blasted through me. If I spent too much time around him, I was going to need to carry a fan. I wanted to run my hands through his rumpled brown curls and get up close and personal with his fit firefighter bod.

Willow Brook had firefighters everywhere. Yet, not a one had done a single thing for my hormones. Until Hudson. With him, my hormones were going crazy like they'd never seen a man before.

I managed to breathe even though my pulse was bouncing around like an excited pony just let out to pasture when I stopped beside Hudson. Seeing as I'd run over his crutches, I thought I needed to be gracious.

"Do you need help out to the parking lot?" I asked as I glanced up.

I had to crane my neck to meet his gaze. He was easily a foot taller than me, maybe more. He was definitely tall and strapping, as the cliché went.

His lips curled at the corners in a slow smile. "I was just about to leave, but I can walk myself."

"Oh, okay," I squeaked. "Let's walk out together."

I told my hormones to calm the hell down. They didn't need to behave like an overeager puppy every time I got close to Hudson. I managed to walk like a perfectly normal person beside him out to the parking lot. Everything was going just fine. Until we reached his truck.

I was trying to be helpful. "Do you want me to get your door for you?"

I blamed it on his smile, the way his lips kicked up at one corner first, the way his eyes twinkled with a sly glint of amusement, and his rumbly voice when he said, "I appreciate it, but—"

My stupid hormones were just going wild inside, and I could barely focus. With that enthusiasm shoving reason out of the way, I reached for his door handle. My boot heel caught on the gravel and I tripped, falling right into Hudson. When I collided with him, my momentum threw him off-balance and he stumbled backward into his truck, his crutch clattering to the gravel.

In a hot second, he had curled one arm around me to keep me from falling to the ground. The end result was me plastered against him with his arm around my waist and his palm splayed over the upper curve of my bottom. My hormones were ecstatic. They wanted more than just a look at his body, and they sure had it. I could feel every delineated inch of his muscled chest.

I was breathless when I looked up into his intense eyes. "Oh, my God! I'm so sorry!"

He stared down into my eyes, smiling a little bit. Heat pooled in my belly as butterflies took flight inside, sending tingly sparks scattering through me.

"Definitely no need to apologize." His low raspy voice sent a shiver chasing over the surface of my skin with goosebumps rising in a prickle all over.

When I managed to get myself together and step back, my breath was shallow and rapid. I tried to order my pulse to slow down, but it was a pointless effort. "I promise, the next time I see you, I won't drive over your crutches and I won't fall on you."

Hudson chuckled. "I don't mind if you do."

With that, I scrambled up some kind of composure, babbled something polite and climbed into my car.

I was just about to drive away when I rolled down my window. "I need your phone number, so I can call you when I get your crutches tomorrow."

Hudson recited it, and I tapped it into my contacts, texting him quickly to confirm. *This is Stella.*

When I stopped before turning out of the parking lot a moment later, my phone vibrated. I couldn't resist looking down at the screen where it sat face up in my console. *This is Hudson.* 😉

The next morning, I had a little chat with my hormones and explained that I knew how things went when I let them—my hormones, that is—run the show. I was going to keep it together around Hudson. My hormones shrugged and laughed at me.

I picked up his crutches and texted him that I was dropping them off at the fire station because I had a meeting. I *did* have a meeting, but I was also being a coward and trying to avoid him.

Later that day at the office, my phone vibrated. I spun it around.

Hudson: *I'm taking it personally that I didn't get to see you when you brought my crutches.*

Thank you for reading Tish & Griffin's story! Want a glimpse of the future for them? Join my newsletter to receive an exclusive scene.

Sign up here: https://BookHip.com/WDCZMPP

p.s. If you are already subscribed, you'll still be able to access the scene.

Up next is in the Wild Fire Series is When We Dare.

**What could go wrong when my brother's best friend becomes my roommate?
I'm about to find out.**

When I met Hudson Fox, I drove over his crutches. Way to go, girl. My hormones think this hotshot firefighter is all that and then some.

My hormones have a terrible track record. They are cheering for Hudson, but my brain knows better. I'm a smart woman with plans and none of them involve romance.

Until I move into my new place and Hudson is my roommate. Complete with Butter, his cat.

Don't miss Stella & Hudson's intense, protective, and emotional romance!

One-click: When We Dare - due out January 2025!

For more swoony romance...

This Crazy Love kicks off the Swoon Series - small town southern romance with enough heat to melt you! Jackson & Shay's story is epic - swoon-worthy & intensely emotional. Jackson just happens to be Shay's brother's best friend. He's also *seriously* easy on the eyes. Shay has a past, the kind of past she would most definitely like to forget. Past or not, Jackson is about to rock her world. Don't miss their story!

Burn For Me is a second chance romance for the ages. Sexy firefighters? Check. Rugged men? Check. Wrapped up together? Check. Brave the fire in this hot, small-town romance. Amelia & Cade were high school sweethearts & then it all fell apart. When they cross paths again, it's epic - don't miss Cade's story!

For more small town romance, take a visit to Last Frontier Lodge in Diamond Creek. A sexy, alpha SEAL meets his match with a brainy heroine in Take Me Home. Marley is all brains & Gage is all brawn. Sparks fly when their worlds collide. Don't miss Gage & Marley's story!

If sports romance lights your spark, check out The Play. Liam is a British footballer who falls for Olivia, his doctor. A twist of forbidden heats up this swoon-worthy & laugh-out-loud romance. Don't miss Liam & Olivia's story.

ACKNOWLEDGMENTS

Thank YOU. Really. For reading, for sharing your love of my stories and characters with the world and with me. Authoring can be a lonely world, and it's readers who make it worthwhile. To the readers and influencers who shout out their love of romance far and wide, I am so very grateful, along with many authors. We all need a little love and escaping into a story is a lovely place to find it.

Gracious thanks to my editor who gets the first pass (after I make my eyes cross with too many reviews of each draft) and kindly helps me make the story better. Many thanks to my proofreader who scouts out the minutiae and patiently reminds me about timelines and such. Hugs to my early readers who let me know about any lingering errors. Any remaining mistakes are mine alone and deserve to be there after that much persistence.

Huge thanks to Najla Qamber for the covers for this new series and making them so beautiful!

To my sweet dogs who are a huge part of my writing journey and to my family for being there. To DBC for all the things.

xoxo

J.H. Croix

FIND MY BOOKS

Thank you for reading All The Afters! I hope you enjoyed the story. If so, you can help other readers find my books in a variety of ways.

1) Write a review!

2) Sign up for my newsletter, so you can receive information about upcoming new releases & receive a FREE copy of one of my books: http://jhcroixauthor. com/subscribe/

3) Like and follow my Amazon Author page at https:// amazon.com/author/jhcroix

4) Follow me on Bookbub at https://www.bookbub. com/authors/j-h-croix

5) Follow me on Instagram at https://www.instagram. com/jhcroix/

6) Like my Facebook page at https://www.facebook. com/jhcroix

———

Wild Fire Series
All The Afters
When We Dare - due out January 2025
Fake It True - due out April 2025
Fireweed Harbor Series
Make You Mine
Dare To Fall
Be The One
One More Time
Wait For You
Ever After All
Light My Fire Series
Wild With You
Hold Me Now
Only Ever Us
Fall For Me
Keep Me Close
With Every Breath
All It Takes
Take Me Now
Meant To Be
Dare With Me Series
Crash Into You
Evers & Afters
Come To Me
Back To Us
Take Me There
After We Fall
Swoon Series
This Crazy Love
Wait For Me
Break My Fall
Truly Madly Mine
Still Go Crazy

If We Dare
Steal My Heart
Into The Fire Series
Burn For Me
Slow Burn
Burn So Bad
Hot Mess
Burn So Good
Sweet Fire
Play With Fire
Melt With You
Burn For You
Crash & Burn
That Snowy Night
Brit Boys Sports Romance
The Play
Big Win
Out Of Bounds
Play Me
Naughty Wish
Diamond Creek Alaska Novels
When Love Comes
Follow Love
Love Unbroken
Love Untamed
Tumble Into Love
Christmas Nights
Lodge Series
Take Me Home
Love at Last
Just This Once
Falling Fast
Stay With Me
When We Fall

<u>Hold Me Close</u>
<u>Crazy For You</u>
<u>Just Us</u>

ABOUT THE AUTHOR

USA Today Bestselling Author J. H. Croix lives in a small town with her husband and two spoiled dogs. Croix writes contemporary romance with sassy women and alpha men who aren't afraid to show some emotion. Her love for quirky small-towns and the characters that inhabit them shines through in her writing. Take a walk on the wild side of romance with her bestselling novels!

Places you can find me:
jhcroixauthor.com
jhcroix@jhcroix.com

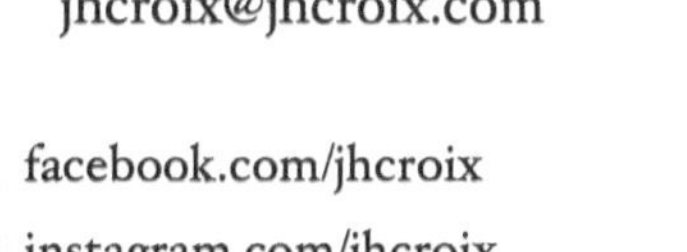

facebook.com/jhcroix
instagram.com/jhcroix
bookbub.com/authors/j-h-croix